PRINCE OF
GREED

PRINCES OF SIN:
SEVEN DEADLY SINS SERIES

K. ELLE MORRISON

Editing by Caroline Acebo
Proofreading by Norma's Nook Proofreading
Cover Designed by Cassie Chapman at Opulent Designs
Interior page design by K. Elle Morrison

Kellemorrison.com

Print ISBN: 979-8-9852047-7-3
Ebook ISBN: 979-8-9852047-6-6

To my slow burn girlies. This one's for you.

DEAR READERS

This book contains material that may be considered inappropriate for readers under the age of 18.

These materials cover:
Graphic sex between consenting adults.
Depictions of death and loss. Elements of religious trauma.

Please leave a review ;)

OTHER TITLES BY K. ELLE MORRISON

Blood On My Name
Audiobook:
Blood On My Name

The Princes of Sin series:
Prince Of Lust
Prince Of Greed
Prince Of Sloth
Prince Of Pride
Prince Of Gluttony
Prince Of Envy
Prince Of Wrath

The Black Banners Series:
Under The Black Banners
Dagger Of Ash & Gold

To stay up-to-date on upcoming titles, bonus material, advanced reader opportunities, and so much more visit Kellemorrison.com to join the newsletter!

For all upcoming projects and updates from K. Elle Morrison please subscribe to the *FREE* Newsletter!

Kellemorrison.com
Linktree

I

STOLAS

Sitri grinned down at his hand across the table. The pot was overflowing with ancient jewels, stacks of money from around the world, and sets of keys to cars and townhomes.

We'd been drinking, smoking, and gambling for hours, and only three of us were left at the table in the private casino room. Ezequiel had taken his leave with a human he had brought for company. Without their constant cooing and flirting, Sitri was more alert and had won the last two hands.

"It looks as if you have run dry, brother," Orobas balked from beside me, his tell.

He had nothing, but the pot was full of my gold and cash.

Between the three of us, Sitri likely had the best hand but was giving no indication if he would fold or hold out to see what Orobas would wager.

"I have a few tricks up my sleeve, don't you

1

worry," I said. "What will you be betting? Your chips are gone, your pockets are bare, and your fingers have been stripped of their adornments."

I flicked my fingertips over the edges of my straight flush, waiting for the sweat to begin to pool at his temples.

He shuffled through his cards once more, a timid smirk on his lips. "I have something that might be of interest. Especially with Sitri's new fascination with human women."

Sitri didn't look up from his cards or acknowledge the remark. His recent run-in with the human Orobas spoke of was still a fresh wound that not many dared to mention. Our fellow prince of Hell had given his heart too quickly and foolishly, and when the action wasn't returned, he had been consumed by it. This poker game in Las Vegas was a product of that thwarted love affair. But my brow perked at the item Orobas was betting.

"You have found an ancient being trapped inside of a human as well, brother? Are they a dime a dozen this millennium?" I quipped.

Orobas scowled and flipped me off, bringing a hearty laugh from Sitri. It was the first time I had heard him laugh the entire trip.

"I have had my fair share of human companionship for the next thousand years," Sitri said, rolling his shoulders and looking between the two of us. "But I would find a place for her at the club. We tend to lose track of our bartenders when they are too pleasing to the eye."

"She was payment for a favor many years back," Orobas said, "but her utility is quickly coming to fruition. You likely know her father, Sitri. An elected official who had a dirty past that was partly formed at The Deacon several years back. His only child in exchange for a seat among the country's most powerful. She could be used for much more than a bargaining chip tonight." Orobas' eyes danced over his cards once more.

"Just hers?" I asked as this was unusual in soul bartering.

"He has a way with fine print." Orobas shrugged, not admitting that he had been outsmarted by the politician.

"All right," Sitri agreed. "Lay down her soul and let's get this over with. I want to head down to the bar before it fills with the undesirables of the city." Sitri sighed.

Orobas held out his hand and a blue flame ignited. He dropped it into an empty whiskey glass and slid it into the pot, knocking over a stack of bills that spilled over a layer of jewelry and gold coins.

Sitri cleared his throat and shifted in his seat before laying his cards down. It was a poor showing, just 5 high.

Orobas burst into laughter and slapped his pair of jacks on the table.

"You are terrible at this game!" he teased and

turned to me. "Show me your hand so I can collect your cars and riches."

He leaned back in his chair, his hands clasped behind his neck to cushion the large head he had developed.

I scrubbed my hand down my face, and the three-day stubble scratched at my palm. "Fine."

He cursed and threw his arms in the air when he realized that his hand had lost the pot.

Sitri and I hooted our laughter at Orobas' indignation. He was not only the Prince of Gluttony but of counting his chickens before they hatched.

"Fuck the both of you. Cheats. Filthy swindlers, the lot." He crossed his arms over his chest and watched as I plucked the glass from the pile to examine it.

The puddle of whiskey roaming the bottom of the tumbler moved from side to side as I brought it up to eye level.

"Whose daughter was worth your misfortune?" I asked. The human's soul captured in Orobas' flame wiggled and squirmed in its confines. It was as if it knew it was being handled by its new owner.

"Senator Harris Gerhardt of California. On the path for the next national election. Evelyn's soul was one of three that he offered for my most treasured favor."

"Does she know?" Sitri stood and slipped on his leather jacket, readying for another strut through the hotel bar.

"In a manner of speaking? No. But she's had the pleasure of meeting me." Orobas flourished his hand vaguely to the room, then got to his feet to join our brother.

With a snap of my finger, the cash and trinkets before me dissipated into the void and to my home in Santa Monica. I set down the glass and watched the flame flicker a moment more, trying to decide whether I should join my brothers or inspect my new prize for myself.

Sitri clapped my shoulder, breaking my concentration. "Come on, Stolas. I wager by the end of the night, we could collect far more than a few new souls. You can play with your new toy tomorrow."

Sitri was right. There was no urgency.

With a wave of my hand, the glass was transported to the safety of my home.

Either Orobas had conned me into accepting a useless human soul or it really was a prize worth the bragging rights. There was no use in worrying over it when I could easily double or triple my soul count in the bar or the casino.

I followed them out of the private room, and we reached an elevator filled with a drunk and giggling bachelorette party.

The bride-to-be eye-fucked Sitri the moment the doors opened.

The curve of his lip and the silent exchange between us told me that he was about to ruin a wedding and entrap the pretty young thing, all in one fell swoop.

The Prince of Lust was on the prowl, flanked by Greed and Gluttony. Las Vegas spread its legs and begged for us to ravish it.

A banquet for the wicked.

A city crafted for the Princes of Sin.

2

EVIE

My father's new wife's name popped up on my phone screen. She'd been texting me all day about a fundraiser she was heading. This call was to remind me of the time I was supposed to be there, but each message was heavily laced with guilt and obligation. He needed an appearance from the lone survivor of the heart-breaking boating accident that took my mother, older brother, and younger sister thirteen years ago.

If it hadn't been for the inner tube I'd been in when the speedboat hit the rocks, I wouldn't have had to dress up like a living memorial for fundraising events.

The coast guard had responded within minutes and hoisted me from the water, but often I wished they hadn't. Some nights, I could still hear my mother screaming out my brother's name. His body was lost to the ocean and never recovered.

Every benefit or fundraiser was another opportunity for my father to rehash the tragedy and reassure his constituents that he was still a family man. Though, the trail of ex-wives he was leaving up and down the Californian coast was more toxic than the plastic floating just off the state's shores. I ran away to London for university after private prep school, but I hadn't been able to get a foothold in the marketing industry after graduation. Without Daddy's money, I was forced to move back to Los Angeles.

The reemergence of his one and only living child had stirred his campaign advisors to thrust me into the spotlight as often as possible. I agreed on the condition that he paid for my apartment and car. Los Angeles was expensive. I was working full-time at one of the top ad agencies and still barely making ends meet. If I was going to be paraded like a show pony, I wanted the prize money for it.

The event Rebecca was blowing up my phone over was Friday night. It was five days away, but every minute counted when you were the wife of a future presidential candidate.

I hadn't seen the dresses she had picked for me, but I had no doubt they all were meant to age me down by about seven years. My father was getting older but wanted to keep his voters under the illusion that he was a spry man with progressive ideals.

That meant that I couldn't look my age.

When approached by other politicians I had

known most of my life, I was always offered the same dusty compliments: "You have grown into such a beautiful woman," or, "Your mother would be so proud to see you now," or my favorite, "I can see you got your father's wits but your mother's beauty."

Constant reminders that I was merely a relic from a time when my father had been young, happy, and had it all. He'd enjoyed the attention of being a single father and widower until I turned sixteen. That was when A-line sundresses, kitten heels, and decorative hair clips became my permitted party attire.

I didn't want to deal with the schedule Rebecca had come up with or the expectations she was passing from my father down to me. I didn't have anything against her. As far as stepmothers went, she was the most tolerable. But she was only eight years older than me—another reason I had to appear younger than I actually was. Daddy couldn't have the media connecting the dots that his wives were getting younger when he wasn't.

I ignored Rebecca's call and went back to mindlessly scrolling social media while the TV lit up my bare living room. Posts from a group of my old friends at a nightclub downtown showed up, and the caption from one of the girls snagged my attention.

Living life as high as I can.

Rhomi Polus was front and center, her phone held out to capture the chaos behind her. Several other people were in the blur of bodies and colored dance floor lights. She would consider herself an influencer, but she was just as much of a trust fund kid as I was. Her father and mine had put on several fundraisers together, but her lawyer father never bothered with politics because money got him much farther than a voting ballot ever did.

The club tagged in the image was only a couple miles from my apartment, and for a moment, I thought about getting off my couch and finding a dress to throw on. But sitting at home was far more comfortable than crashing a night out with near strangers.

I hadn't seen Rhomi in ages, but we kept up through random messages and commenting on photos or status updates.

A pang of feeling left out hit me.

I'd left more than just friends in London. I'd left Muhammad, or Mads, as he preferred.

We hadn't been dating for long when I decided to return to the States. It had only been a few months, but he was already focused on a new job that had a promising future. One that wasn't centered around his personal life or me.

I opened up the text thread that he and I had sparsely used since I left. The last message from him was dated last week. "I miss you."

I didn't answer. I couldn't.

I missed his smile. I missed the way he made me laugh. I missed the way he made me feel. But I couldn't admit that I missed *him*. Not after the fight we'd had that solidified my choice to leave.

So instead, I scrolled up to a photo he'd sent me last month. It was finally warm in London and he had been at coffee with a few of our friends. The photo of the four of them holding up their takeaway cups came after a selfie of him enjoying the sunshine. The warm glow of his skin and the dark curls over his brow sent me retreating into myself.

I wrapped the blanket around my shoulders a little tighter, pretending that I wasn't utterly alone. Pretending that I could be out if I wanted. That I could be at a nightclub flirting with all manner of men in this city.

But the shallow lie proved nothing except that I wasn't.

Rebecca sent through another text, and not a moment later, she called.

I finally answered.

Maybe it was to stop her incessant calls, or maybe to allow a voice other than mine into the room for a brief moment.

"What's up, Becky?" I greeted her with a name I knew she hated.

She sighed but pushed on. "Your father wants you to come to lunch tomorrow to go over the agenda. Are you free around one?"

"I have to work," I reminded her.

"You still need to eat. Come up to the house. I'm making egg salad."

I cringed. I was sure it was by my father's request that she was making one of the foulest foods I could think of.

"Fine. I'll be there." I didn't wait for her to respond before I hung up.

Impulse rushed through me, and I shot off two texts.

The first was to my father.

ME:

> Next time you want me to come over, invite me yourself.

Typing bubbles popped up on his end, but I swiped out of that conversation and into my social media feed.

I clicked on Rhomi's photo and typed a message.

ME:

> Hey, girl! Want to grab coffee tomorrow?

I took a deep breath and set the phone down on my thigh. I didn't expect her to respond right away, but I fully expected my father's response to be immediate, condescending, and cold. But the *ping* that followed wasn't from my texts. It was from Rhomi.

RHOMI:

> Yes, babe!!! I'd love that! Alfreds in Westwood Village around 10 a.m.?

See you then!

Favolosa!

I smiled to myself and ignored the text that followed from my father. Coffee with another human being in a city I should love would satisfy the isolation for a while.

I turned off the TV and made my way back to my bedroom through the kitchen when something out of the corner of my eye sent ice down my back.

My heart leaped into my throat.

The kitchen was empty, but I could have sworn I saw the shadow of a man leaning against the sink.

I ran to my bedroom and locked the door behind me.

It was nothing.

I was on the top floor of a luxury apartment building. No one could have gotten in without me knowing. I took a deep breath and sat on the edge of my bed. My ears were pricked for any sound coming from behind the door, but the apartment was silent.

I was alone.

3

STOLAS

The sun rose over Sin City in a lazy, hot haze. Two human bodies dozed next to me. One was a woman from the bachelorette party we crashed, and the other a man she had taken a fancy to when we got to the bar. His wedding ring had been tossed across the room in a drunken display last night and now lay on the floor.

Liquor had loosened his tongue in a confession of never being with another man, but the prospect of getting to fuck the young woman and be shared was too much for him to pass up. A quick promise that what happened in this bed would stay here, with his name in exchange, was all he needed to suck my cock while being pegged by our lovely bed companion.

She, a high school biology teacher, on the other hand, had made no such deal. Her soul had no shame upon it for what she wanted. No weight of insecurity lay on her when she rode my face to completion while getting her ass eaten by the tech salesman from Scottsdale. I would have liked to keep her around a bit longer, but with no name or promise, I had nothing to hold her by.

There was a knock on the door and I slipped out of the bed to answer. Sitri leaned against the frame, a cocky smile on his lips as he looked past me to the mess I had untangled from.

"I was wondering what sort of trouble you found. Just two? Losing your touch, darling," he teased.

"We can't all be blessed with he stamina to entertain a whole wedding party then fuck them all," I replied. "Quality is sometimes more interesting than quantity."

"I don't believe you for a moment. Anyway, I have to see Lucifer then get back to The Deacon, care to come along?" He pushed off the frame and straightened the hem of his shirt.

I glanced back. Though I relished human embarrassment by the light of a new day, I was bored of Las Vegas and had wanted to go home days ago. I cleared my throat loudly, startling the man from his blissful sleep. He looked down to the school teacher then searched for the being who had filled his throat and ass the night before. His eyes honed in on me and Sitri at the door and his cheeks flushed deep red.

He scurried out of the bed, dropping to the floor to search for his clothes as quickly as he could.

"There's no need to be bashful," I said, his eyes snapping to me from his belt in his hand.

"No . . . I just. I have a conference several blocks away," he shuttered out as he slipped his slacks up his bare behind. His boxers hung from the ceiling fan, out of his line of sight.

The woman still in the bed stretched and sat up. The cream sheets sloped down her soft, dusky curves and her bare breasts graced the room with her satisfied dreamy expression. "Good morning, puppy."

He glanced around the room, avoiding her naked body. I leaned down and picked up his discarded promise and held it between my fingers to show him.

"You dropped this last night before you plowed into our friend, but not before you buried your face in her tits." I winked.

He tripped over himself to get to me with his hand outstretched. I dropped the copper circle into his palm.

"She'll never know, right? You promised." His pitiful plea brought a smile to my face.

"Of course, Carl. She will never know." His shoulders relaxed at my dark voice and his expression softened to a dreamy relief.

"Last night was"—He looked from me back to the bed to the naked woman now on her knees— "incredible."

She winked at him, sending him back into his panicked escape. His pale face became as pink as a pig's backside. He pulled the rest of his clothing into his chest and scooted past Sitri and me. His eyes stopped on each of us for a moment before he headed to the elevator, not daring to look back again.

Sitri huffed his amusement and swung his attention back to the woman on the bed. "By chance, do you know how to tend bar?"

She giggled and brought a knuckle to wedge between her teeth, "Sorry. Not my specialty."

"Pity," he returned.

"Give me an hour and I'll meet you at The Deacon," I told him before he nodded and disappeared into the void.

I turned back to my remaining bedmate from the evening. She was pulling her dress up her body and settled the straps on her shoulders. I went to the end of the bed to sit and put my shoes on when she leaned down and kissed me softly on the cheek.

"Thanks for the wild night, handsome," she said, fingering the straps of her high heels and leaving without a second glance.

The door closed and the void swallowed me up. A moment later, my living room appeared around me. The windows were full of sunlight and the view of the ocean. The kitchen table was laden with my winnings from last night, including the glass tumbler that was alight with the blue flame of my new soul. Her father would be a useful component to a plan I had been ruminating on for years.

Whether Orobas knew it or not, he had given me the key to a fortune I had been thirsting over.

Being a prince of Hell granted me the gift to inflict ferocious greed upon the human race, but the power over legions of lesser demons and a few millennia of bartering human souls was fruitless and ash on my tongue.

I wanted to grip all of creation in my hands and squeeze until the pulp seeped through my fists.

I had the ability to instill greed, need, and covetousness in others, but their selfishness would not gain me my truest desires. It all had to be done in small steps.

In my other demonic brothers' endeavors, they were free from any strings that bound them to the influences they produced. They also lacked the drive to dominate.

They weren't greed incarnate.

I didn't only have the urge to have it all. I had the itch over my skin and bones to grab anything and everything that I could and mark it as my own. The constant frenzy for more was what captivated me— just like the flesh of humans and demons captivated my brothers.

The seven us crowned in princely duty had been given unique battles to contend with. Becoming the embodiment of a sin was a power unmatched by any other angel or lesser demon.

But there was a fallback to every one of our abilities.

Orobas, Prince of Gluttony, could not and would not ever be sated of his cravings, no matter how much he indulged. Though he could give mortals of all their luscious worldly wants, he was doomed to seek out anyone or anything to feed his hunger until time stopped.

We were not so different in that way. It was why we got along and gravitated to one another.

Sitri, however, had found a way around the curse that was incidental to his throne—if he didn't drown himself in his own misery.

He was once potent enough to bring down kingdoms. To inspire lords and ladies to place seeking pleasure and lust over their duties. They would offer him all their riches for just a small dose of his favor.

I'd always admired him for the ease with which he used the most carnal of human desires to build his empire. While he focused on his businesses in Los Angeles, his reach was global. Every major city was a mainline to Sitri's pockets and consistently equipped him with more souls tempted by the sins of the flesh.

It had finally dawned on me that if I was going to use my own gift to bring me the world, I would need to appeal to the masses. I could not do that myself. There would be too many questions about my agelessness and murky paper trail. And Lucifer would never allow me to reign on Earth as he did in Hell or our Father did in Heaven. But with a human puppet to dance in front of the camera and use for my platform as a headpiece, I could finally be suffused with the power and influence I desperately needed.

I shifted the dancing flame in the glass and watched the base bloom and wilt with the movements of air around it.

Evie's father would be a fine puppet, and what better way to get close to Harris than to get his daughter in my pocket?

4

EVIE

"Evie! Over here!" Rhomi was standing at a table inside the coffee shop. She had sent me a text that she was there early, but I was also running early.

I hadn't slept much after the startling shadow in my kitchen. The dreams I'd had were too vivid, and I had woken up at the crack of dawn drenched in sweat.

The coffee shop was busy, with plenty of people picking up their orders and bustling around. After putting in my order for a large caramel latte with an extra shot of espresso, I made my way to where Rhomi stood facing the large window.

She smiled brightly and threw her arms around my shoulders.

"How have you been, girlie? It's been years. Didn't you move to France or something?" The apples of her cheeks were pink and full with her warm smile.

"Yeah, I've been back for a few months now. I should have reached out sooner."

"Oh, honey, no worries at all. I'm so stoked to see you and catch up." She giggled and nudged the top of my hand with her manicured fingers.

"I think the last time we saw each other was two summers ago," I said. "When our dads did that summer park cleanup fundraiser."

She rolled her eyes. "Fuck my dad and his fake caring-for-humanity bullshit. I haven't let him drag me to one of his phony events since. That was when Kip Spokes pushed me into the buffet table and shrimp cocktail flung all over my dress. Hate him." She flicked her wavy brown hair over her shoulder in indignation.

I wasn't sure what to add to the conversation, but the barista saved me by calling out my order.

"I'll be right back," I said, but Rhomi was already digging through her purse and pulling out her phone.

The barista smiled and gave me a quick nod when I reached for my coffee. I took a deep breath and fought the urge to fake some kind of emergency.

What was I thinking when I asked Rhomi for coffee?

We didn't have anything in common, even when we were younger. She was flirty, talkative, and always the center of attention, whereas I preferred the company of smaller groups. I didn't mind dancing at clubs but was typically along for the ride when it came to going out with our friends.

I walked back to her, and she set her phone down and smiled again.

"Okay, so tell me about Europe. Did you meet anyone special?"

"I loved it there, actually. I'm sad I had to come back, but it was hard to find a job in London."

It wasn't a lie, but it also wasn't fully the truth. I'd had a job before I left but didn't have the stability my colleagues had and was laid off within a few months of starting.

She didn't cut in to speak; she just chewed on the end of her paper straw and focused her dark eyes on me.

So I went on spilling my guts to a practical stranger. "I was dating someone but we decided the distance wouldn't work. But maybe someday we'll find our way back to each other, you know?"

She nodded along, a pitied pout on her bottom lip at my supposed European love affair gone wrong.

"What about you?" I asked, eagerly shifting the conversation back to her. "Are you dating anyone?"

She'd have tons to talk about until I could peel away to my father's house for lunch and chalk up the outing to a failed attempt at rekindling friendships over coffee.

"I don't do commitment, but I have a few regular hookups here and there." She winked and shimmied her shoulders playfully. "Actually, one of my sneaky links just texted me an invite to The Deacon Saturday night. Do you want to come? I can totally put you on the guest list. She's DJing and on the verge of making it big."

"Saturday night?" I picked at my cuticles, unsure if I should make up an excuse to stay home on one of my only evenings off work.

"Whatever your plans are, dump them. I promise you won't regret it. The Deacon is a life-changing experience."

"What's The Deacon?" I was unsure if she was part of some Hollywood-BDSM-Jesus cult.

"It's a club. Very hard to get into without knowing someone. I mean, you should be thanking me on your knees for the invite, to be honest." She giggled, but the joke wasn't lost on me.

"I don't know. That doesn't sound like a scene that I'd fit into," I said with a playful laugh, hoping she'd take the invite back.

"Don't say no, Evie. I refuse to hear it." She waved her hand about, swatting away any doubt in the air. "I'm getting there around 10 p.m., so if you get there after that, text and I'll come get you."

"All right . . . I guess . . ."

She was already tapping her thumbs over her phone screen.

"I just sent you the address. I have to run, but I *will* see you soon. Don't stand me up, okay." She smiled carelessly while she gathered up her purse and coffee before adding one last instruction. "And this is a very exclusive club, so wear your hottest outfit. You never know who you'll meet."

She pressed the tips of her fingers to her lips and blew me a kiss before dashing out the nearest door, leaving me dumbfounded.

———— ⬥ ————

Rebecca met me in the driveway when I pulled up to my father's house for lunch. I was twenty minutes late, and she was pacing the freshly power-washed pavement.

"Where have you been?" she said through a passive-aggressive, toothy smile.

She didn't want to sound too angry in front of the catering staff bringing in tables and chairs from two white vans.

I closed my car door and shook the ice in my second latte of the day. "Traffic," is all I gave her before walking past her and through the front door.

The high, arched entryway housed a life-sized portrait of my father with his three children. Our mother had been excluded for the comfort of one of his ex-wives when the painting had been commissioned.

I hated that painting.

It was there for my father to milk every bit of pity from the media when campaign season came.

I fidgeted with the locket at my neck, the same one I wore in the portrait. It was my mother's.

Before the accident, it had held two tiny photos: one of her children and one of her parents, who had long since died.

Now, the locket held nothing but the ghost of one of my mother's most prized possessions. It had been too hard on me for it to carry the faces of the family members I had lost, but being able to touch the smooth surface on the back that was etched with her initials and the diamond-studded flowers on the front kept her with me.

After the quick pause for my reminder of constant grief, I walked to the kitchen where my dad sat at the marble island with his laptop, cellphone, and tablet.

"Hey," I greeted him on my way to the fridge.

"Evelyn. I'm so happy to see you, kitten. How's work?" He looked up briefly then picked up his tablet to silence the news video he had been listening to.

"Fine." I rummaged through the many foil-covered platters and grabbed a shrimp cocktail cup.

I set it down in front of me on the island and waited for him to finish tapping on his phone.

He had to put all other parts of his life on hold to be able to focus on the family that supposedly came above all other duties.

Another lie, but how else would he be seen as a hardworking father if he didn't spend most of his time buried in his devices?

He finally set the phone down, closed his eyes, and took a deep sigh. He was in casual clothing, so he must have worked from home to prepare for the event. His light-blue eyes surveyed me a moment, then he smiled warmly. It was a glimpse of the man I had always wanted as my father—before duty and his hunger for power had washed him away.

The character he played for the world was the man I'd wished for growing up.

The reporters spun stories about him being home every night to tuck me into bed or missing trips abroad to go to my ballet recitals, but none of it was true. He would show up to my field hockey tournaments randomly, a news crew close on his heels. The only nights he was home before nine was for our monthly family dinner, a tradition that only continued so local restaurateurs could claim he was a regular.

Putting all of himself into his community was how his career started over twenty years ago, but his deep-pocketed friends and business associates were how he had kept his position for so long and moved up in the governmental hierarchy. He hadn't announced his candidacy for president yet, but the storm of preparation had started years ago. He was smart and calculated every move he made. Every relationship he cultivated was just another pawn for him to play eventually.

"I appreciate you making time for us on Friday night. In the next few months, I might need you on the campaign trail. The core family unit is the backbone of this country after all," he preached, but his charm was wasted on me.

I looked through the large kitchen window behind him. Rebecca was telling the rental company which path to take to the backyard. Her bouncy, blonde curls whipped around her face in the wind.

"You'll have Becky with you. Why would you need me?"

He looked after his wife leading two men hauling equipment on dollies, then back to me and for just a second, I thought I saw his eyes roll.

I might have been projecting, but I'd seen the small crack before when one of his previous wives began divorce proceedings. He was never the one to file, but he knew exactly how many extra hours to work and how little to communicate in order to drive women away.

I didn't know exactly why my father did this, but he was becoming as regular as the tide.

Rebecca was decent as far as my father's relationships went. I had a feeling she valued her role at my father's side more than she valued her marriage. A chance at being the First Lady was far more titillating than the alimony she would win in court.

"Rebecca is good company and one of my pillars

of support, but I could not imagine traveling for months without seeing you," he said, a kind smile masking his true intentions.

"I can't miss work. But if you give me an itinerary, I'll see what I can do."

This was enough to end the subject. That and Rebecca bustling in from the backyard.

"They forgot two of the tables but will bring them when they bring the chairs tomorrow morning. The decorator should be here in the afternoon with her crew." She continued her report with only mild irritation lacing her words. "They will just have to start on the strings of lights and buffet tables until all the tables and chairs are in place."

My father nodded along but didn't bother to add anything.

I dipped a cold shrimp in the spicy cocktail sauce then bit down, savoring several more before the end of Rebecca's droning about her list of tasks.

She finally turned to me. "I need you to go upstairs and pick which dress you're going to wear. In your room. On the bed."

"Rebecca has chosen several that will look beautiful on you. Keep the rest. The receipts are in the garment bags," my father added, knowing that the hundreds of dollars he spent on them would be going into my pocket in the next few days when I returned the hideous things.

She shooed me up the stairs. Her voice followed

me up until I reached the guest room that had been deemed mine.

A light-pink calf-length dress had been laid at the foot of the bed. Lined up at its hem was a pair of white, short-heeled shoes.

Ugly.

The combination reminded me of the church outfits my nanny would force me into every Sunday morning.

Pass.

The other dress was purple—maybe more eggplant—with a pair of black heels.

I held it in front of me. It wasn't skimpy, but there had to have been a mistake. There was no way my father would have approved this dress around so many of his donors. The hem landed at mid-thigh, and the neckline was curved. Not enough for a scandal, but I was never one to look a gift horse in the mouth.

I grabbed it up along with the others I hadn't bothered to consider and headed back downstairs.

"Find one that fits the occasion?" my father asked over his shoulder.

"Yeah, I think so." I hiked up the armful of garment bags. "I have to head back to work. I'll see you Friday."

I gave him a peck on the cheek and dashed out the door before Rebecca could rope me into any other expectations.

5

STOLAS

"**A**nd look who has finally graced us with his presence," Sitri shouted across the empty club.

He and Ezequiel were bantering back and forth over a bottle of liquor, the oak bar top between them.

Sitri stood stacking glasses for his barbacks while Ezequiel lounged uselessly on a stool. He and I had never gotten along, but since he'd taken his position as Sitri's right hand, I'd had to deal with him much more than I preferred.

Orobas was nowhere to be seen, but I knew he was lurking around. He would never miss the opening of the VIP floor we had invested in.

I scoffed. "Has it gotten so dire that you will be tending bar tonight, brother?"

"Foolish man. I have recruited several beautiful

humans to pour tonight," Ezequiel answered. "Of course, only about half will survive the weekend."

He smirked at Sitri, sharing the moment of cruel humor. The walls of the club were lined with secrets, and its rooms, hallways, and passageways led individuals into realms of endless darkness. The hidden rooms were used for spur-of-the-moment seductions between patrons and demons. The hallways could lead someone into the arms of a toxic stranger for the night if they were feeling lonely enough. The abyss, on the other hand, was not used as often as I thought it should have been.

What better way to torture the scum of the Earth than trapping them with only their own mind to keep them company?

"The employee turnover is going to start the rumor mill." I sat on a stool a few feet away from Ezequiel, and Sitri slid a glass of something pink and fruity toward me.

"You worry too much," the Watcher said, not at all putting my worry at ease. "This industry is full of fair-weathers who'll neither call nor show up for their shift for the opportunity to follow the latest pop singer on tour. That's the beauty of Los Angeles."

The Deacon was more than just a nightclub and investment. It was where, on any day of the week, desperate souls could be harvested. People clambered for just one moment of happiness and freedom on the dance floor. For the chance to meet a stranger for a one-time tryst to recount at parties.

The nightclub was also a place for the princes of Hell to converse on an even field.

Yes, Sitri was the owner and main operator, but it was one of the last demon establishments that hadn't been dismantled by our holy brothers for giving us an unfair advantage. The Soul Armistice was strict in that way. The agreement made between the remaining Holy and the Fallen stated that humans had to willingly give into their sinful urges, but our demonic influence was protected at The Deacon. Humans were entering of their own volition to commit whatever sins they had set out to commit for the night.

Countless rumors swarmed about The Deacon being a place where Hollywood starlets and other high-profile clients could let loose without being bombarded by paparazzi. Sitri had security at every door and private entrances for his most esteemed guests. The more common patrons signed NDAs at the door, and their phones were checked along with their coats. Every measure imaginable was taken for a simple night without consequences, except for the ones that daylight would bring.

On this particular night, Sitri and his staff were getting ready to open the VIP section he'd been renovating on the second floor. He had the opportunity—after a near apocalypse—to remodel, place additional wards against angels, and upgrade the soundproofing in some of the hidden pleasure rooms.

"Who is on the guest list for this weekend?" I asked into my glass, not at all caring who answered.

I scowled at the sour, perfumed liqueur.

Sitri laughed and replaced the glass in my hand with one filled with top-shelf smoked whiskey.

"A few supermodels, influencers, a human prince and his secret lover—you'll never guess who it is— and Seere has alluded to making appearances," Sitri answered.

"What a night it will be," I said. "Gluttony and Wrath in the same room mixed with alcohol and the highest of snobs. I hope you hired extra security for the night."

I smirked, knowing he didn't. He loved the chaos that our most lethal brothers caused.

He returned the mischievous smile and chuckled. "It will be a disaster to remember."

"That it will," Ezequiel chimed in, "but there is still more to be done."

He got to his feet and, with a dramatic tip of his head, finished off his drink.

I rolled my eyes as he stalked off to busy himself with whatever it was he thought was his business to attend to.

Orobas swaggered out from an opening in the far wall. He seemed to be alone, but his ruffled hair told a story that he hadn't been for very long.

"Ah, Stolas. Just the brother I wanted to see." Orobas bellied up to the bar next to me. "I have a rather boring party to attend on Friday evening, and

I thought to spice it up, I'll introduce you to Evelyn Gerhardt. Her father is throwing a fundraiser, and I've secured us an invitation."

I perked a brow at him. "Owning his family's souls would garner you a prime spot on the guest list, I'd imagine."

"Want to come, Sitri?" Orobas turned to Sitri, who wrinkled his forehead at the invitation.

"I'll pass," Sitri returned. "Soggy crab cakes and flat champagne surrounded by dull humans sounds like a waste of a Friday evening."

"Plenty of wicked mortals to bargain with, though," Orobas said. "There is always a bright side, my most tantalizing brother. You just have to be willing to work for it."

Orobas had never had to work hard for anything. Harris Gerhardt still owning his own soul was proof enough of that. He had willingly sold members of his family for his own gain, but according to Orobas' vague explanation, Harris had retained his own.

I was grateful that Sitri was uninterested in attending the senator's party. It would have been far too easy for him to seduce Harris. Where the sin of gluttony might have failed, it was unlikely that lust would.

Plus, being introduced to Evelyn would save me the time of contriving a meeting.

6

EVIE

It had been days of long nights at the office and sneaking away on my lunch breaks to shop for an outfit to wear to The Deacon. Nothing I owned would be up to Rhomi's standards, but there wasn't a store in the mall for highly secretive dance clubs. I'd finally given up and resigned myself to faking my own death and deleting all my social media accounts if I didn't find anything by Saturday afternoon.

Perhaps I was being a tad dramatic, but it shouldn't have been so hard to find an outfit.

I thought of my siblings often, but more so when I was stressed over social engagements.

Would my sister have been able to find the perfect little black dress? Would my brother have been the one our father wanted at his side at parties? Would my mother have stood up to my father about the ridiculous outfits and restrictions he set for his daughter?

I added those questions and too many more to the bottomless pit where I kept the rest of my memories.

Missing them came in waves, even all these years later.

On Friday evening, as I dressed, I thought back to the last party my parents had thrown. Our mother and father had been on the phone all day. My siblings and I had been dressed up and shuffled around by our mother, who took each compliment about our appearances or gentle natures and attributed them to our father's hand in raising us.

When the ghost of my family had quieted and my hair was perfectly starched, I headed downstairs to where my father and Becky were waiting. I was quickly sent to welcome guests as they arrived.

"You look lovely tonight," said a faceless, balding man with a younger woman on his arm.

"Thank you, and welcome," I answered and directed them and another two couples into the house. "My father is so pleased you could make it this evening. He is in the living room."

After what felt like hours later, I was relieved of my duty and was free to roam around until I could genuinely say I had met every guest and could slip out without being noticed.

Becky and my father cornered diplomat after diplomat in the living room, their toothy smiles plastered on their faces as they schmoozed. I had no choice but to mingle and would never get away with hiding upstairs in one of the guest rooms. Becky had made sure they were all locked after I'd gone missing at a party and my father had given a toast to his family. I hadn't been there to look misty-eyed.

A round-faced CEO of a banking firm cornered me near the finger foods. I was ten minutes into listening to him tell me the current stock rates when a man caught my eye.

Actually, two men.

I knew one was Oro, a business associate of my father's. Oro made my skin crawl and vibrate all at once. The way he looked me up and down felt thick and slimy.

"I'll be seeing you," he had said in his deep, gravelly voice the last time I saw him. Then he'd shared a knowing look with my father that set every one of my hairs on end.

Now, he was standing with a man who looked as if he had been carved from marble by the gods. His dark hair was teased and gelled to the side. Not one strand looked like it dared to be out of place.

The short stubble on his jaw darkened his features, but his sapphire eyes blazed from across the room to me.

No.

Through me.

This beautiful man couldn't have been looking at me.

The room around me went still in the lifetime I spent staring back into his depths. But when he looked away, back at Oro, my stomach dropped, and I was forced to swallow down the disappointed whimper that had amassed in my chest.

7

STOLAS

"Evie, there you are. I was just looking for your father." Orobas' toothy grin affronted the young woman he had pointed out as my poker-night prize.

The curtain of her party smile slipped for the briefest of moments when she saw who had called her name. Orobas didn't acknowledge the momentary loss of her hostess persona and drove forward on his mission to introduce me to her.

"Oro, good evening," she answered and peered through the crowd for her father. "I just saw him with the CEO of Solar Star."

Orobas and I knew better.

Harris Gerhardt was upstairs with the head of his young wife between his legs for a quickie. The self-serving cad would be done any moment. The thrill of a house full of guests was too much.

"I'm sure he'll find us in a moment. Busy man,

your father." Orobas turned to me, his smile devious before he looked back at her. "This is my brother and business partner. I don't believe you've had the pleasure of meeting the senator's daughter Evie."

"It's nice to meet you . . ." She politely waited for a name to use.

She belonged to me, but giving her my true name would give her the power to summon me if spoken just right.

I let her dangle on the silence for another moment before deciding that it was only fair that I leveled the playing field.

"Stolas," I said, gifting her with the social reprieve of my name.

"Stolas," she repeated, the first and last letters getting caught in her teeth and dragged along her tongue like silk. "That's a . . . strong name."

"Suits him, doesn't it?" Orobas chimed in, clapping my shoulder. "Handsome devil." His bouncy tone did nothing to rid her expression of its curiosity. "My glass is empty, bad luck at such a fancy affair. I'll be back in a moment."

Her hostess senses slipped back into place. "Oh, I can—"

"No, please stay and occupy my brother," Orobas said. "He has been bored to tears and I need a rest from carrying the conversation for the both of us." He scurried away before she could answer.

She watched after him a moment before turning back to me, surprise still on her face.

When she caught my eyes wandering over her features too long, she stiffened but didn't make an excuse to run. She pulled the corner of her lip between her teeth and tapped her fingernails against her champagne flute.

"You don't want to be here, do you?"

Her shocked expression didn't recover as quickly as it had before. "Uh, well." She laid her hand over her chest and clutched a small oval locket that hung from her neck, shielding her discomfort from my blatant accusation. "I'm not really a fan of large gatherings, but my father and his associates are so kind and generous that I enjoy meeting and mingling with his supporters."

I smirked at the plastered smile she tried to fake. "You're a terrible liar."

She covered her mouth to stifle her laughter, but a small snort escaped between her fingers.

"Fine," she admitted. "You're right. I'd rather be home in my sweats watching trashy TV and eating my weight in ice cream. But when Daddy needs me, I come."

If she played her cards right, she'd be calling *me* daddy as I made her come undone.

I had to restrain myself. Her sweet laugh and luscious curves sharpened my tongue and dirtied my humor.

"You must be close to your father to give up more exciting plans to be put on display for these bloated windbags."

She considered me for a moment. Her previous apprehension was long gone, and her lips curled into an easy smile. "Tell me what you really think, why don't you?"

I cleared my throat, aware I may have been too outwardly disgusted by the humans assembled. They wore some of their greatest sins on their sleeves.

"Forgive me," I said. "My brother is the social one for a reason. I usually deal with numbers and figures. I'm only dragged out to parties when more complicated agreements need to be made."

Her eyes widened while she mentally sized me up and found me her equal and a worthy distraction. She finally released the bite of her tongue.

A small thrill rang through me.

"There's nothing to forgive. I'm just surprised to meet someone as cynical as me at one of these things."

The sight of her father and stepmother drew our attention to the archway near the staircase. He'd spotted us, and his brow knitted with worry when his eyes locked on mine.

He knew who and what I was.

Though he made his deal with Orobas, I had been given an explanation after my winning hand in Vegas. A scorch of heat and bitter anger tipped my tongue. There was a deep circle of Hell for humans like him who made deals with demons for other humans' souls.

While most of my brothers viewed the deals as a two-for-one sale, I saw it for what it was.

Dirty and despicable.

But he would have no idea yet that Orobas had relinquished his hold over their deal to me.

"Would you like to see the garden?" Evie's rebellious voice brought me back to our previous conversation. "My stepmother worked so hard on it, but hardly anyone has made it out there. It would be a shame to waste the fruits of the landscaper's labor."

I could see she was hopeful for an excuse to wander away.

"After you." I raised my glass and followed her to the garden.

Hundreds of misty white lights were strung above the stone patio. Tall, thin topiaries wrapped in twinkling fairy lights bracketed the walkway that led out to a large fountain that spilled down into a coy pond.

Evie stopped and sat down on a stone bench near the farthest end of the pond. Classical music from in-ground speakers helped drown out the lingering chatter of the crowd coming through the open doors. It was a balmy night for Southern California. The rare looming rain clouds threatened overhead but would likely travel south or out to sea before a drop made landfall.

Evie took a drink from her glass and sighed. "As much as I hate to admit it, the garden looks beautiful."

I slipped one hand into my pocket and peered down at her. I had given her space, but the goose bumps on the tops of her shoulders were begging me to come closer.

"I would give anything for my mother to be the one throwing these parties. Or my brother to be the one ushered out to shake the hands of the rich and annoying," she said, her eyes adrift in the night lights and memories of her lost family.

She'd give anything to have her mother. If she were anyone else, I would have had an advantage —a tall, dark, mysterious stranger who could grant an impossible wish in exchange for a piece of herself that she would hardly miss until the end of her life.

"I'm sure my father has recited the story to you, but my mother, sister, and brother died in an accident. Always gets him the sympathy votes."

I did know the story but nodded and gave a sullen frown. "It sounds as if your mother is still well-loved and missed."

She smiled down to her lap then lifted her gaze to meet mine, sadness welling behind her soft features.

"And I'd bet her choices in wine and hors d'oeuvres would have been much better," I finished.

Her gentle laugh eased away her heartache and lured her into the comfort of a stranger.

"She wasn't much for wine. But she could mix up one hell of a batch of margaritas . . . or so I'm told."

"That is a skill I admire," I said low and watched her inch closer.

There was a moment of silence between us, a transition from the deep that had been consuming her world to the shallows of the present.

"It must be nice working with your brother," she said.

"He understands me in ways most others wouldn't. Being brought up the way we were makes connections outside of our family difficult to maintain. It's easier to stick together." Not a lie, and a truth she would likely wish she still had.

"That's nice," she said with sincerity. "How many siblings do you have?"

"Dozens." Another truth, but this one perked her ears.

"Are you serious? What, were you born in a cult?" She wrinkled her nose and snickered.

"You could say that." I shrugged then took a long sip of my drink.

"Wow. That's—"

"Exhausting," I finished for her. "But I tend to keep up with my closest six brothers regularly."

"Well, sure. With a family that big, you'd have to pick your favorites. Though for Oro to be one of the close ones, the others must be insufferable."

I let the amused huff from my chest reach my face. "He has nothing but kind things to say about you."

"Wonderful. Was one of the comments on my

eye color because as far as I know, he's only ever looked at my chest when speaking to me." She rolled her eyes but gave a quipped, crooked smile.

She was witty, and from what I could tell from this conversation, she was kind. Not exactly what I had been expecting from the daughter of a snake politician. She had known privilege but had retained a level head. Trauma would do that for a human. Getting close to her in order to use her as the weapon to coerce her father into becoming my puppet was going to be more pleasurable than I had initially thought.

I crouched down so our faces were level, but her eyes fell to my lips.

"I'll remind him how beautifully green they are. Like polished jade." I spoke slowly, wrapping intent around each word to stir the butterflies in her stomach.

She held her breath, dragging her gaze up to mine for longer than she'd likely intended, before bolting to her feet and smoothing out the wrinkles from her dress.

The moment was too much, and she had obligations as her surviving family's trophy.

"I should make the rounds. Thank you for taking in the fresh air with me, Stolas. Enjoy the rest of the night." She stretched out her hand to bid me farewell.

I straightened myself and took her hand but

rotated and brought it up. "I hope we meet again soon, Evie."

Our eyes locked as I lightly caressed my lips over her knuckles.

Her cheeks flushed and her mouth opened, but it seemed that her words were lost. Instead, she nodded and walked away.

I waited until her silhouette had disappeared into the house before slipping through the void. I had no desire to mingle with any other mortals now that my agenda to encounter Evie had been accomplished. I knew the impression I left her with would have her thoughts trailing back to me throughout the rest of the night.

I also knew that we would meet again. Soon. I would make certain of it.

8

EVIE

After hours of peering over my shoulder, to catch sight of Stolas, and shaking hands with politicians whose eyes felt as if they were all over my skin, I found my father in the kitchen hovering over a tray of crab cakes and chugging a glass of water.

"I'm going home," I said, grabbing my bag from where I'd stored it in the private liquor cabinet. "Your wife is passed out in the bathroom."

"Damn it, Evelyn, you just left her there?" He looked out into the living room and waved over a waiter.

"She's not my responsibility, Dad. Maybe the next one will be able to hold her liquor. But you're getting pretty close to women who aren't legally allowed to drink."

He barked an order to the waiter and one of his staffers to assist Becky upstairs then turned around, massaging his temples. The deep lines on his forehead were exaggerated by the strain of his fingers.

"I don't need your smart mouth tonight, kid," he replied with a sigh. "Fine, go home and be safe. I don't need the media scrutinizing your driving after a fundraising event at my home."

Another reminder that my safety came second to his campaign image.

"I promise not to run any red lights or ram pedestrians on Wilshire Boulevard."

He rolled his eyes and then pulled some painkillers out of a small medicine bottle.

"Goodnight, kitten. Love you," he said, wrapping an arm around my shoulder and kissing the top of my head. He bustled out of the room.

"Night, Dad," I said to no one but myself.

<hr>

I got back home unscathed but replayed every awkward encounter I'd had while driving. I rode the elevator up while recalling the conversation I'd had with the public defender who'd taken it upon himself to inform me that I had "developed into a fine woman," and he wished he were twenty years younger so he could have asked me out on a date.

Twenty years still would have been far too old for

me. He had been "old" since I was a child and was easily forty years my senior. The look on his wife's face had almost been enough to encourage me to empty my stomach right there on the family room floor.

It wasn't an occurrence that I escaped often. Every old man who knew me growing up or knew my father felt like they had some perverted right to ogle the woman who had grown from the young girl they once knew.

I shook off the visceral stain that had been left on my skin and shimmied out of my dress to get in the shower. The whole evening hadn't been awful. I'd gotten a chance to run into a client from my company and connect with them on a more personal level. Any foothold was a good one, and he had set up a time for the two of us to meet and discuss working more closely. Was it poaching? Probably, but management would see it as valuable customer relations building.

Then there was Stolas.

The mystery man. I hadn't seen him at all after leaving him in the garden. Oro had been talking with my father when I'd made it back inside but had also departed shortly after. I thought I had caught sight of Stolas out of the corner of my eye a couple times, but when I turned to look, he was nowhere to be seen.

There wasn't anything concrete I could describe about the way he'd behaved while we lingered at the edge of the party, but there was something in the way he looked at me and the smile on his lips.

Not overly flirtatious or forward.

Casual. Confident. Comfortable. Cunning. Cultured.

How many other cheesy *c* words would I think of to describe him? But none of them really caught the essence of those few minutes when everything around us melted away and his full attention was on me.

Just me.

Not my name or connections through my father. Not the ghosts of my past or the obligatory sympathy I garnered by simply existing when so many of my other family members did not anymore. Even when I brought my mother and brother up, he hadn't given the run-of-the-mill responses I typically received. He didn't offer an apology for a crime he didn't commit. He hadn't looked away in shame for still having all of his dearest and most loved people still alive and in his life.

He'd just . . . stayed. He stayed in that moment with me, and though he hadn't known more than my name thirty minutes earlier, he had provided a safety I hadn't felt since being with Mads. I missed that familiarity more than I actually missed Mads or our relationship.

I shook myself from the moment we stole in the garden. Overanalyzing and focusing too much on the way he looked into my eyes would have no positive outcome. And putting more emphasis on one compliment than he'd likely meant had my chest shrinking like a giddy schoolgirl with their first crush.

I promised myself that I wouldn't think about him, but having to remind myself while I showered that his words meant nothing was still thinking about him . . . wasn't it?

After getting into bed and taking some melatonin for good measure, I drifted in and out of sleep for hours. The image of his lips grazing my skin resurfaced over and over. It was the briefest of moments. The quickest of touches. Still, I couldn't shake the feeling of butterflies in my stomach or the skitter of goose bumps over my arm.

Stolas haunted my dreams with images that hadn't happened but felt just as real as his hand had felt in mine: blurred flashes of him tracing my curves, soft, pouty lips warming my neck then chest. A soft caress of his palm at my back drew me in closer. A firm grip on my waist, then fingertips that dug into my bare hips, his head between my thighs to bring me to climax.

It was still dark when I woke up in a cold sweat and had to shake the eerie sense of being watched from the shadowy corners of my room. My stomach was full of nervous energy and a queasy tremor to the point that I checked my temperature. I had convinced myself that I was experiencing a delirious fever from food poisoning or a mysterious virus.

I was sick, but not physically.

It was a frenzy that I would have to drown out with mind-numbing paperwork followed by a night of excessive drinking—if I ever finished this report in time.

It was Saturday, but filing and emails had to be done before Monday. I hated wasting my weekends, but if I didn't do it, my work would never get done.

My boss was reasonable most of the time. He had hired me before he realized who my father was, and he never treated me like the trust fund baby most of my coworkers saw me as. Someday, I would be funded by my father's estate, but not until he had made his blazing dash for the White House.

I enjoyed my job and the team I had been placed on for the most part, but I tried to keep every facet of my life in its own little box. It was to protect myself from anyone who would want to get too close and see that I was a mess of old family trauma.

The constant work and obligations from my father kept me too busy to do much of anything else anyway, including moments with tall, dark strangers in fairy-lit gardens.

And there it was again.

My brain wandered back to the memory of Stolas' lips on my hand for about the hundredth time that morning. The spark ignited to a blaze that shot up my arm and raged a storm in my core.

When the heat sank lower and caused a throbbing ache between my legs, I forced myself out of yet another distracting cloud.

How could his lips over my skin feel like they'd set my soul on fire?

Between actively trying to stay busy and my face getting so hot, I worried I would pop a blood vessel or melt my eyeliner off, I was fantasizing about whether or not I'd ever see him again. If our paths would cross at another fundraising event, or maybe on my father's campaign trail.

Not that I would know what to say or why I wanted to be near him again so badly, but I was making up scenarios and would-be conversations in my head nonetheless. We would find an empty corner somewhere with a bottle of wine to split between us. He'd joke about his brothers, and I would tell embarrassing stories from when I was younger and would scare my nannies half to death by hiding in closets.

I would laugh at his jokes, allow the wine to go to my head and feel playful enough to touch his arm or chest. Then I'd lean in to tell him a secret just so my lips would graze his ear. Maybe our cheeks would touch and the stubble of his chin would rub against my skin. Our eyes would meet. We'd share a breath. Then, after the rest of the world had slipped into darkness, our lips would touch and my entire world would be torn to shreds because that moment would end too soon.

Damn it, Evie. Snap out of it!

I needed fresh air to clear my head of the alternate universe I had created in my head of his hands slipping up the hem of my dress and his fingers exploring me until I was breathlessly moaning his name . . .

A walk outside wasn't going to be enough, but I locked up my office anyway and started down the street toward the coffee shop at the end of the block.

9

STOLAS

I didn't have to wait long. I knew after the night of restless sleep I'd invoked, she would be in the need of an afternoon espresso.

When Evie came in, she didn't look around in her desperation for caffeine. She ordered quickly, careful to thank and tip the barista with cash, then moved down the counter where white paper cups with black lids were being shuffled out to waiting hands. Her fingers twisted the locket around her neck while she waited.

Her eyes flitted up when she heard her name called.

She turned to go—cup in hand—and her gaze finally landed on mine.

Her eyes darted around, likely looking to see if she was imagining me or if anyone else saw the man she'd been thinking and dreaming about since last night.

She must have decided she wasn't hallucinating because gave me a small, casual wave. I returned her greeting with a nod and a coy but welcoming smile.

Instead of waiting for her to think too long and talk herself out of coming over to me, I got to my feet and closed the distance between us.

"This is a pleasant surprise," I said, practically feeling her shiver at the sound of my voice.

"It is?" She laughed, her cheeks pink.

My lips pulled into a warmer smile, inviting her shoulders to relax.

"I mean, it is," she corrected and brought her coffee to her mouth, biting on the thin plastic to mask her surprise.

"What brings you to this side of town?" I asked to break the silence.

"I had some work stuff to do. My office is at the end of the block."

I nodded.

"What about you?" she asked.

"Believe it or not, I come this way every couple weeks for comedy lessons."

"Comedy lessons?" The surprise in her tone lifted something in my chest and brightened her face.

"The prestigious Pauly Shore's Comedy for Dummies. We meet every other Saturday morning." I winked, giving away my joke.

She laughed. She tucked a loose lock of hair behind her ear then hid her smile behind her fingers.

"I'd say they're paying off."

"I'll pass along the review to Pauly." I leaned in for a mock whisper and brushed my fingers over her forearm, which erupted into goosebumps.

It was a distraction for a sleight of hand to catch something dear to her. Her nostrils flared, and her pupils dilated as she caught the scent of my cologne.

I pulled back to slip my hand in my pocket, but not as far as I'd been before.

The heavy pause between us allowed her to soak up my presence.

"You're coming from work?" I asked. "On a Saturday?" Inserting myself in her waking world would solidify the hold I was digging into her.

"No rest for the determined." She gave me a half smile. "I'm still trying to prove myself within my team, which means extra hours on the weekends."

"They're not paying attention if they don't see your dedication," I agreed, but our ambitions were clashing at the moment. "Do you ever get free time?"

"Not often. I have plans tonight, but I typically have the waking hours of an elderly woman in Boca. The coffee is for longevity."

I gave her my best panty-dropping smile then took a long sip from my coffee cup. I ran my tongue slowly over my lips. Her eyes widened as they followed the movement.

"Would you consider going to dinner with a new friend if it was at an early-bird-special hour?" My voice broke her focus, and she looked away with another flush to her cheeks.

"If they didn't mind having dinner at five thirty on a weekday, then I would give it a shot." She gave me a cool smile, but the bright delight in her eyes said more than she was willing to say out loud.

"Monday?"

Her bottom lip twitched as she thought it through. After her dreams and the constant onslaught of thoughts about me, she wasn't keen to scurry off so quickly. Like a cool sip of water on a scorching day, we savored the satiety of her thirst.

"Okay. Monday."

I took my phone out and unlocked it, and she rattled off her phone number. Instead of just saving it, I sent her a text with the name of the restaurant I intended to take her to—the one with a rooftop bar that her stepmother and her father frequented with their friends in local government. With the right encouragement, we'd catch them at the tail end of our meal.

Her phone dinged a second later. She ignored it but watched my hand slip my phone back into my pocket. Her eyes caught on the tattoo on the inside of my wrist.

My sigil.

"That's an interesting tattoo. Does it mean anything?"

"It's a family thing," I answered.

One would say it was a map. Or a blueprint for much more than I had bargained for with my contribution to the Fall.

I held it up for her to see fully, and I watched her fingers timidly trace the lines, loops, crosses, and circles. When she'd had her fill, she ran her fingers through her hair. "Do you have any more tattoos?"

"Yes."

I didn't give her any further details. I wanted to let her mind wander.

The pink across her nose and cheeks deepened.

Seeing her squirm under the heat of the question sent a thrill through me. I wanted to feel her nails digging into the owl's wings across my chest as she rode my cock and moaned my name.

That time would come, but until then, I needed to keep her guessing.

"I should get going." I cleared my throat and took a step toward the door. "Enjoy your night, and I'll see you on Monday."

"Oh," she said, trying to mask her disappointment, "yes. See you on Monday."

With one last smile, I headed out the door.

Once the coffee shop was out of sight, I held up my prize: her locket. A zap of energy had loosened the loops of the chain, and the pendant had slipped into my hand while her attention had been elsewhere.

I slipped into the void to deliver the charm to

Haniel, the alchemist. The locket was the perfect item to enchant and present to Evie as a beacon in a couple days. By then, the desperation Evie was stewing in would make her more pliable to my plans for her father. Until then, I was expected at The Deacon.

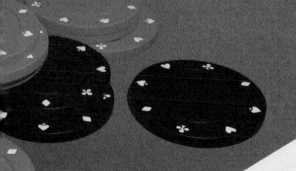

IO

EVIE

9:15 p.m.

Was it too early to round the corner and wait outside the club?

I was parked a block away, expecting the distance to be worse than it was. I'd been ready for hours and had forced myself out the door and into my car before I chickened out.

Running into Stolas at the coffee shop was a sign that I needed to stop manifesting awkward encounters. That was the only way I could explain the coincidence. That or he was stalking me.

Right, because that beautiful man would be stalking me after one quick conversation.

It wasn't so far-fetched. People did crazy things, especially here in L.A., and my father was high profile.

I shook the thought from my head.

Stolas had no way of knowing that I had been

dreaming and thinking about him so intensely. The fact of the matter was the run-in was a coincidence, and the heavy weight in my chest was from the anticipation of having dinner with him on Monday.

Though he hadn't clearly labeled it a date, I was going to assume it was one until he started grilling me for information on my father's campaign or business holdings. The longer I thought about the invitation, the more my stomach knotted and my fingers itched to text him and cancel.

Out of habit, I reached for my locket. I'd cried for an hour in my car when I realized it was gone, and retracing my steps had led me nowhere but back to my empty office to finish paperwork and emails.

I peered down at my phone screen and opened up one of the three social media apps I scrolled through to dull my senses and pass the next forty-five minutes. New posts from friends in the UK appeared first. Three of them were together on a walkabout in London. Mads' handle was tagged in one of the corners as the photographer, but several thumb pushes later, I saw his own version of events on the outing. He was sitting on a park bench, holding the largest sausage roll I'd ever seen in his lap that he was gesturing to crudely.

Penis jokes.

Did I really miss penis jokes?

When I clicked on his page, there were several new posts that I hadn't allowed myself to see from the past weekend. In one of them, he was shirtless at the gym; he was fitter than when I'd left. Probably because any time he mentioned going, I would suggest a walk together instead. Those walks always led us to a restaurant or pub. I cringed inwardly. It wasn't that I didn't like exercise or feeling accomplished after a good workout. I just found a pint and chips more satisfying.

I closed the app, stopping myself from the spiral that would surely come if I let myself dive too deep. I'd wasted just enough time; it was a few minutes to ten o'clock.

I sent a text to Rhomi and got out of my car to wait.

ME:

I'm walking up now.

Her reply came through almost immediately.

RHOMI:

Be there in 2.

I rounded the corner and saw a tall bouncer leading a group of four people into a door that I hadn't noticed before. Two cars pulled up to the curb and another group piled out with squeals of excitement. They were escorted into the building, and the two cars drove off as I crossed the street.

I was alone again in a part of town that felt as if it shouldn't have been empty. It was rare to find any street in Los Angeles without a car or person lingering, but here I was, standing in front of some super-exclusive club in the dark.

This was how my episode of a true-crime podcast would start. I could already hear the voices of two middle-aged women telling my story and joking about the purple cat sweatpants and matching sweatshirt I had stashed in my car. They would probably call it a tragedy for my father, just like the rest of my family. I wondered if he'd be president by the time they released their take on my life.

Before the exit music started in my head, a car pulled up and Rhomi stepped out first with two other people close behind her.

"Evie!" Rhomi's shoes stampeded over, and she wrapped her arms around me. "You look so hot."

She loosened her grip around my neck and turned to her company. The taller of the two who'd emerged from the car tipped their driver then gave out a loud hoot of excitement.

"Is this her?" she said, looking from me to Rhomi. "She's gorgeous. I thought you said I would be the only hot and single one here tonight."

She crossed her arms and pushed out her bottom lip in a mocking pout. There was nothing she had to worry about. Aside from the fact I was obsessing over a man I'd only met twice, she was flawless. She fit every beauty standard on social media. With long legs, a cinched waist, busty chest, and undeniably beautiful face, she would have men on their knees, begging for her to step on their balls, no matter who she was with.

"Oh, stop. Self-deprecation is your only bad quality." Rhomi rolled her eyes but grabbed her arm to pull her closer to us.

"This is Tiffany. She's going to be the next Oscar-winning actress." Rhomi reached a hand out to the second friend she brought and pulled them to her other side.

"And this is Jordan, my NB darling who works three jobs and never sleeps. They're also the hookup for all the hottest clubs in Los Angeles, including The Deacon."

Jordan smiled, wrapped their arm around Rhomi, and landed a kiss on her cheek. "Quit bragging about us and let's go in before we get rejected for loitering."

I felt out of place among Rhomi and her friends. Tiffany's dress looked more expensive than my car, and Jordan effortlessly pulled off the casual goth-hippie look in all black with a leather jacket and boots. Out of all of us, Jordan would be the only one comfortable after an hour of dancing.

The dress I'd found after returning my discarded Rebecca-chosen ones was nice. It was black and strapless. The essence of the "little black dress" was in its simplistic nature. I hadn't bothered with a jacket since it was close to seventy degrees at dusk. The most troubling element of my outfit was the choice of heels. My red-bottom stilettos would have me crying in the morning for sure. I wore heels to work often, but not nearly this high and thin.

Rhomi was dressed more casually than I expected but still looked glamorous. Her short skirt was layered over a pair of black stockings, and her tank top bodysuit hugged her curves and pushed her chest up and out on display.

"All right, all right, but we have to go over ground rules first." Rhomi untangled herself and fluffed her hair. "Tiffany and Jordan already know, but they need a reminder because they break them all the time."

She scolded her friends with a scrunch of her nose. "Rule number one, keep your drink number to three or less. We don't get sloppy. Rule number two, don't leave your drinks with anyone but us. Rule number three is the most important: we come together; we leave together."

"No Black Dahlias on our watch," Jordan chimed in, and a chill ran up my spine at the imagery.

Surprisingly, I felt safe with the three of them. I hadn't been sure about what to expect going out with Rhomi. She was the poster girl for the L.A. party scene but had obviously seen or even been a victim of the drawback of being a young, fem-presenting person in a city that was known for chewing us up and spitting us out when we hit thirty.

Out of the darkness, the tall bouncer I'd seen escorting other patrons cleared his throat.

Jordan flashed a smile and something small and black from their back pocket, and the bouncer nodded.

"You all ready?" the bouncer gruffed, obviously tired of the monotony of his job.

"We are!" Tiffany called out and took hold of my hand without any hesitation.

"Here is your stub. I will take your cell phones and IDs. You won't be needing either while inside. The bar is cash only, so take what you need from your purses and wallets now before depositing them in the locker."

I shot a look to Rhomi, who was digging through her purse to take out a few hundred-dollar bills and stuffing them in her bra.

"We have to lock up our purses?" I asked low, so only she heard me.

"It's against the rules to take photos in The Deacon. Don't worry if you didn't bring cash. My treat."

I swallowed the knot in my throat. Being in a strange new place without my phone to keep me company or for any type of emergency had me grinding my teeth.

"Miss?" the bouncer said, holding out a clear plastic box for me to deposit my possessions in.

Rhomi put her things in first, and I followed. If she felt safe doing this, then maybe I was being overly sensitive. Jordan and Tiffany did the same without hesitation, and the bouncer handed each of us a small slip of paper with a locker number and a barcode.

"If you lose your stub, you'll have to wait until last call to retrieve your things. Understood?" he barked.

We agreed in unison then watched him turn and begin walking, not worried that we wouldn't be on his heels. With Jordan and Rhomi in the lead, we followed the bouncer into the door that had been hidden in the shadows. He paused only a moment to lock our belongings in a wall of black lockers with a scanner under each handle. I took a deep breath and buried my anxiety.

Moving deeper into the club, the bass from the DJ booth assaulted my eardrums before my eyes adjusted to the dark hallway we were being ushered through. Rhomi's grip on my right wrist and Tiffany's hold on my left made me part of the lifeline as the tunnel opened up onto the massive dance floor.

The Deacon was like no other club I'd seen. Black drapes hung from the ceiling, sectioning off parts of the room and creating pockets of inner corners where dancing could be one of the many activities that were going on. The most light came from the DJ booth, where flashing strobe lights pounded along with the beat of the music. Rhomi's hookup—I assumed—bobbed up and down and side to side. Her hands were in constant motion to orchestrate the show and electrified the air with her musical masterpieces.

Though it was too dark to be sure, the sounds of pleasure rang out between song tracks. I squinted through the red and white laser lights, but with the blur of bodies and constant movement around me, it was hard enough to keep myself on my feet while being dragged toward the bar.

Once we made it to the front of the line, Rhomi shouted out an order for a round of shots and slapped money on the bar. The tall, dark-haired bartender held up four fingers to confirm, and one by one, they were passed down our row.

In a quick huddle, Jordan held their glass up. "*Geonbae!*"

"To friends. New, old, and reconnected," Tiffany added then led us in swallowing down the cinnamon-flavored liquor.

The burn settled in my chest, and the warmth spread to my limbs. It didn't take long to become comfortable with the absence of a bag or phone. The situational crutch of technology wasn't needed here. We were living in the moment and letting the outside world trek on without us for a small amount of time.

We were absorbed into the mass of revelry and swept into the undertow. The music filled the air and commanded the sway of my hips. Where uncertainty had been only moments ago was freedom, a taste of what I had been wanting for longer than I cared to admit. I knew no one but the three people who were dancing next to me with full smiles on their faces and mouthing the words to the lyrics without any worry of embarrassment or judgment.

Happiness.

We were liberated from the world outside because it had melted away and been replaced by the pounding bass, strobe lights, and strangers who were only there to let loose.

A hand gripped my waist from behind, followed by a gentle squeeze to gain my attention. The owner of said hand was tall, blond, and gorgeous. He smiled down and said, or maybe mouthed, a request to dance. I looked back to Rhomi, who eagerly nodded her approval. Tiffany's attention had already been stolen by an equally beautiful man with light curls.

I turned to face my new dance partner, and his hands confidently wrapped around my back to bring me closer. His taut body pressed hard against mine. With every move he made, my skin prickled at the pull of the muscles in his arms and torso. I closed my eyes and got lost in him. Lost in the heady moments of his breath in my ear between songs and the twitch of his lips at my temple when my hands traveled up and down his chest and stomach.

He was intoxicating. Everything inside of me was begging to be touched, and as if he could hear my internal anguish, he fanned his fingers up my neck and brought my face up. The club melted away, and we stilled. My eyes bolted open to find impossibly blue ones staring down into me. Deaf to the music, he feathered his lips over mine, not in a kiss but another question.

Drink?

He pulled away once the vibration from his lips ceased for my answer. I nodded and groaned silently when his arms relaxed and his hand slipped down to hold mine. He tapped Jordan on the shoulder to mime to them that we were going to grab a drink, then he pointed to Rhomi and Tiffany, who were too enamored with their dance partners to acknowledge him. Jordan nodded and held up one finger, indicating that they would accept the round of drinks from my mystery man for our group.

Jordan's brows raised as I passed them, my jaw slack from their exchange.

Nice, Jordan mouthed their approval and turned back to the ass that had been grinding against them.

I followed the gentle pull on my hand up to the bar, not willing to let go for more than the sake of not getting lost in the sea of people. If he let go, I would surely crumble in a puddle of sweat and the butterflies in my stomach. That was all I was made of after that dance.

When we reached the front of the line, the bartender's eyes shot to my companion and down to me. Their lips twitched before giving us a subtle nod. They poured an entire tray of shots then slid it down. To my shock, the blond man picked up the tray and held it above his head.

We made our way back to what seemed to be the center of the dance floor, and Rhomi hooted and hooked her arm with mine. The music was still too loud, so she gave me a wink and took one of the offerings. We took our shots together and set the glasses on the tray upside down. Tiffany held up two fingers after taking one of the shots herself and handed another to the man she had been entangled with.

Two. We had two of our three drinks for the night—a reminder that we were here to have fun and not lose the natural high of being young and unhindered. I eyed the remaining shots on the tray then the man holding it. He offered it to me again and I shook my head, wanting to wait and enjoy a mixed drink after dancing until my feet wanted to fall off.

He tilted his head, an obvious look of confusion knitting his brow. I shrugged and declined again. He took one more then passed it to the man with an arm snaked around Tiffany.

Rhomi pulled at my arm to bring my ear down to her mouth just as a song ended. "Let's go to the bathroom."

I nodded as the music started up again. Rhomi motioned to our dance partners that we would be back in a moment. Thankfully, the ache I'd held in my gut subsided the moment she and I practically fell into the bathroom. The door swung closed behind us and my eyes had to adjust to the bright-white lights.

"Oh my God, he is so hot, Evie!" Rhomi threw over her shoulder as she closed a heavy stall door.

I stepped up to the black porcelain sink and took a paper towel from the dispenser. I wet it to pat across my neck and over my chest where my heart was still pounding wildly.

Away from the crowd and constant hammering against my senses, I was starting to feel the ache of my feet from my shoes. The black and white tile would have been cool on the soles, but I knew the moment I took my heels off, that would be it. I wouldn't put them back on, even for the gorgeous man who was so much taller than me.

"They're all way too sexy. What is this place? A modeling agency rec room?" I didn't need a real answer.

An exclusive club in L.A. would, of course, be flooded with the most attractive and powerful people. Rhomi opened up the stall and came to stand next to me at the sink. She washed her hands and touched up her makeup, not one bit mussed from the heat or sweat.

"I told you this place was a whole experience. Are you having fun?" She looked at me through the mirror.

"Yeah." I smiled, my cheeks on fire. "I've been to plenty of dance clubs, but there is something different about this one."

"Something? Or someone?" she teased, knocking my arm with her elbow.

"He is something."

I was still holding on to that melted-away feeling. The stress of my day was long gone.

"Well, remember the rule. We came together; we leave together," she said, drying her hands with a new towel.

"Then I better make the best of the next few hours." I laughed and opened the door to the bathroom for her.

I followed her out but was stopped in my tracks by a face that sent ice plunging into my stomach.

Stolas.

II

STOLAS

hy is she here?
How is she here?

Unlike our run-in at the coffee shop, I didn't plan for this to happen. I'd had half a bottle of whiskey with Orobas in one of the VIP lounges upstairs while humans fawned at our feet. I'd come down to the main floor to get some space from the crowd that had been forming around my brother's influence.

The entirety of the evening I had been picturing Evie's face. Maybe I was hallucinating the drunken mirage of my obsession standing in Sitri's club.

But when she looked around, also questioning the validity of my presence, I knew she was real. She walked with determination to stand in front of me, close enough that I could reach out and touch her—or pin her to the wall next to us and have her gasping.

93

"What are you doing here?" she said over my imagination and the too-loud music.

I'd complained to Sitri countless times that the music was obnoxious, and for a demon to make a proper deal, their terms needed to be heard and agreed to, but now more than ever, I wanted the volume lowered. His solution was the addition upstairs, but I cursed him further in this moment.

"I could ask you the same question." All wit and humor had left me with the surprise of her presence in a demon-owned nightclub.

She grabbed my wrist and pulled me into the less exposed corner near the bathroom doors. I glanced several inches to our right to the hardly visible crease in the wall indicating one of the hidden rooms within The Deacon. Maybe it was empty.

"Stolas?"

Her cheeks and chest were flushed with a sheen of sweat over her sun-kissed skin. For being unsure of her energy level earlier today, she was holding up like any other twenty-something here.

She raised her brow in her impatience for my explanation.

"A couple of my brothers own this club. Orobas and I are investors and were invited for the reopening."

"Investors?"

"That's right," I answered, my shoulders relaxed. "And having deep and pliable pockets earned me a VIP booth. Care to join me?"

It was a bold move. Not as subtle as my last attempt to put myself in her path, but when the prey is within the predator's reach, they become a meal.

She looked over my shoulder, and I followed her line of sight to whom I assumed was one of the friends she arrived with.

"Your entire group is welcome," I insisted, refocusing on her face and bringing her attention back to me.

She wrapped her arms around herself and shifted her weight from one hip to the other as she considered my offer.

"Evie, it's okay to decline. I won't be offended."

Her arms loosened, but not fully. The offer was still present between us.

"Where is the booth? Maybe I'll stop by later."

I smiled, unsure if she was brushing me off or truly torn between her evening plans and the alternative I'd created.

"Upstairs. You won't be able to get in without being accompanied by a VIP."

"Oh."

I wanted her to come with me, but not up to the booth. I wanted her alone. Like when we had stolen a few minutes at her father's party. I didn't want to take her upstairs to Orobas, who would croon and smirk in our direction between shots of liquor from a human's belly button.

She touched the bare spot at her neck, absent of the necklace I had plucked from her at the coffee shop. Haniel had quick hands, but it would be another day or so before it would be ready.

"Who's this?" A voice behind me broke the tension between us.

"This is—" Evie began, but I quickly cut her off, unwilling to share my name with this new human.

"I'm a friend of Evie's father. I was just saying hello," I explained, then I turned back to Evie. "I'll be seeing you soon."

With that, I dipped my chin to both of them and headed back upstairs. I refused to look back and hoped to be able to find her in the crowd through the two-way windows in the floor of my booth. The first thing I saw upon reaching said booth was Orobas seated with a human straddling his lap. His face was buried in the chest of the young woman whose ass bounced on top of him.

I sat down, my knees wide to give me a better view between my feet.

The lights flashed and the tops of heads pushed and pulled with the tide of the music. It would be useless attempting to find Evie among the hundreds of bodies writhing together.

The thought of anyone touching her but me irked my nerves.

"What's the matter with you?" Orobas said, coming up for air.

"Nothing."

"That's convincing," he slurred then took a shot. "You have a scowl on your face that could

96

scare the paint off a bus." He held up another for me to take.

I eyed his hand but took his offering. "You might want to slow down. It's not even midnight and you've lost your senses."

The woman who had just been playing the part of Orobas' drinking vessel giggled and sat up from the low table. She fixed her skirt then sat down to admire the both of us.

He wrinkled his nose, disgusted by my accusation. "And besmirch my title? Brother, some of us cannot rely on our attitudes to spread our gifts to the masses. I am excess. All revelry and misguided fun must be inspired by my hand." His arms flung out. "I am all of this."

"Calm down, brother."

Orobas spun around. It had been Ezequiel calling for Orobas to quit his showboating. Under his arm was a tall blonde woman who was likely a model or actress.

"Hope you don't mind if we join you," he stated.

"It depends. Did you bring anything for the rest of us?" Orobas' eyes roved over the creature Ezequiel was pulling onto his lap.

"Oro," Sitri warned as he came through the crowd. "You'll behave around our guests." He ushered in more people. The last person stole my breath.

"Evie!" Orobas' voice boomed.

Her eyes shot from Orobas to me. My throat

dried to the point that words lodged themselves behind my tongue.

Sitri wrapped his arm around Evie's shoulders and brought her to his side—a prize he would be showing off for the night.

"You didn't say you knew my brother?" Sitri said into her temple.

"I didn't know Oro and Stolas were your brothers," she answered, her voice small and shaky.

"A lovely surprise all around, it would seem," Ezequiel commented next to me, his eyes fixed on me. That disturbing, amused smile of his was on full display. He loved catching Fallen in uncomfortable circumstances.

"Wait, Evie. Isn't this the guy you were talking to downstairs?" one of Evie's friends remarked as they scooted into the booth.

"I say that calls for a toast." Orobas lifted his hand and struck his fingers together to alert the waitress.

"This has just turned into a much more interesting night than I had foreseen," Sitri mused.

The oversized booth easily sat the newcomers in addition to the woman Orobas had been entertaining, though she was more interested in her drink now that Orobas had set his eyes on someone else.

Sitri looked down at Evie then met my eye, and a devilish smile crept up his cheeks when the pieces started to fall into place for him. Ezequiel hadn't been at the table in Vegas when I'd won Evie from

Orobas, but with the way he passed glances from me to Sitri then to Evie, he had realized there was a connection.

A waitress came over with a tray of champagne and set it down at the table. Orobas grabbed up two glasses at a time and handed them out, his fingers brushing over each human. I shot him a look when he sat down next to me. His influence over these humans was more for his own ego than to lighten the mood. And, as if on cue, two of them downed their drinks then reached for another.

"Tiffany. Jordan. Stop, we said only three drinks," the one sitting nearest Evie shouted, but it was too late.

A second glass had been drained, then a third.

Whatever pact they had made was thread thin against the power of the Prince of Gluttony. Orobas smiled into his flute at the bickering.

"Rhomi, lighten up. It's just a little bubbly," the blonde said before laying her head on the Watcher's chest. Her hand trailed up his neck, bringing rouge to her cheeks.

"Well, you didn't have to leave your dance partner downstairs." Rhomi huffed and crossed her arms like a child.

"I'll dance with you, darling," Orobas offered with a flit of his outstretched hand.

Rhomi stood and pulled Tiffany and Jordan to their feet to follow Orobas to the smaller dance floor next to the bar. Ezequiel watched for only a moment before following the sure thing that had been pawing at him.

Sitri wound his finger around a loose lock of Evie's hair. "I should check on the manager. They're new and rather clumsy."

Evie's eyes followed Sitri as he stood and took several steps from us before snapping back to me. She didn't move closer, didn't give away a single thought.

Pinned to the cushion by her stare, I waited for an accusation or for her to start to piece together how staged our meetings had been.

"Are you here with anyone?" she asked, her tone flat.

"Just my brothers." I crossed my ankle over my knee and sipped at my whiskey, hoping for any semblance of calm.

"Why?"

"Excuse me?"

"You're handsome, rich, connected, and seem to be everywhere. Why are you here alone?" She seemed to be examining me as if I were an anomaly to be dissected.

"You didn't come with anyone," I tossed back casually.

"But I ran into your brother."

"Are you saying you came here with the intention of hooking up and have succeeded?"

"No, I—that's not what I said."

"Because perhaps I had the same intention but am not as charming or approachable." I cocked my head and smiled, watching the ice in her posture melt away.

"I doubt that." Her lips tightened, restricting the smile she wanted to return.

She looked around the lounge. The luxury of the VIP booths had spared no expense, and she was meant to be surrounded by lavishness. To be doted upon and never have to ask for anything. Her father had always provided for her, but somehow she had retained an innocence that didn't often come with being raised in the public eye.

I'd been staring too long when her eyes caught on mine then pulled away.

She recoiled with surprise and a small bit of fear when she finally discovered the see-through floor beneath us. "Is that safe?"

"Entirely." I stood and crossed over the pane of glass to demonstrate.

"Can they see us?" Her eyes were fixated on my feet and the party below.

"No." I sat down next to her. "No one can see us."

The weight of my body on the cushion pulled her closer, but she didn't reposition herself. Her eyes had marked my movements then settled where our hips touched before trailing up to my face.

"You look beautiful tonight," I said, settling my arm across the back of the booth behind her. "It's a shame they can't see you. Or maybe it is my great fortune that only I can."

"Is that your attempt at hitting on me?" she quipped. The smirk she'd been holding back surfaced with a giggle that sent my heart racing.

"Not at all." I scoffed and moved in closer.

Her eyes fell to my lips.

"I don't need childish pickup lines or cheesy compliments to show someone I'm interested."

"Is that why you're here alone?" Her cheeks flushed at her own derisiveness.

"I was here alone because no one interested me. Until I went downstairs."

Her lips parted and closed. The quick or witty comeback was lost to the electricity flowing between us. The slow build to a thunderstorm weighed down my chest, making my lungs feel heavy.

I laid my hand on her knee and drew in closer.

"Is this okay?" I asked, catching the notes of rose from her perfume and the musk of the sweat that had dried on her skin.

She nodded slowly, intent on retaining eye contact.

My fingers brushed at the smooth skin of her inner thigh, and I felt the slight tremble of the muscle there.

I made her nervous. I could see it in her eyes and in the way she held her breath.

My palm heated over her skin, and my fingers reached the hem of her dress. I pushed the soft fabric up by only an inch then stalled to give her a moment to push me away or give me any indication that I was pushing her toward a limit.

Her lashes dropped, and her lips parted.

I leaned in, bringing my fingers to her jaw to draw her closer. My neck heated under my collar. I wanted to devour her whole. I wanted to have her gasping my name as if it were the last oxygen she'd ever breathe. Every sense she had would be ensnared by my essence. No craving would be sated or thirst quenched if it wasn't provided by my hands.

As quickly as I could imagine the taste of her lips on my tongue, a voice tore through the thick tension.

"Evie!"

Rhomi. Her words and hands ripped Evie away from me and dragged her up to her feet.

"We have to go. This asshole just tried to shove his hand up my dress in front of everyone," Rhomi shrieked loud enough that several other groups turned around to see the commotion.

Evie looked down at me, an apology on her face.

A rush of anger bloomed in my chest as I searched the dance floor. Orobas was drunkenly stumbling toward us with no trace of remorse for interrupting what would have been a pivotal moment. He blasted an insult to Rhomi then gestured for her to fellate him.

"I—" Evie stole one last glance at me before Rhomi pulled her toward Jordan and Tiffany, who were waiting for them at the top of the stairs.

Orobas sank into the booth across from me, exasperated by the scorn he'd just received. "Prudish bitch. She would have been lucky to have had me for a night."

"In your state, you wouldn't have stayed conscious long enough for your clothes to come off," I scolded, but he shrugged it off coolly. "You owe me for that interruption."

"You should be thanking me. I'd bet good money that she will be pounding on your door within the day to finish what was started."

"Ten thousand," I said through gritted teeth. I was furious and petty.

"Twenty. If she finds you in the next"—he glanced down at his watch then back up to me with a sloppy grin—"twelve hours, you owe me twenty thousand dollars *and* that pretty new sports car you won off Sitri in Vegas."

"You don't even drive."

"No. But you do." His malicious grin sent a sparkle to his glassy eyes.

I huffed. "You really are the worst of us."

"Tell Seere that fact when you see him, won't you? He likes to believe he is the baddest of the bad."

I rolled my eyes and lost myself and the rest of the night in the bottom of a whiskey glass.

12

EVIE

Rhomi's hand around my wrist tightened as we made our way across the first-level dance floor to the lockers. I pulled out my ticket to scan as the music pounded in my ears. It had been much quieter upstairs, and the sudden blast from the DJ booth was causing tension behind my eyes. A migraine was going to be my only companion when I got home. And because of both issues, I was not feeling sympathetic to Rhomi's egregious complaints.

The locker attendant called from the end of the row, but the syllables were lost. I looked over Tiffany's shoulder to see the brother I had been dancing with earlier coming toward us.

He bent low and spoke over the music. "You're welcome anytime."

He handed me a card then turned back, disappearing into the crowd once again.

The small square was void of all color and space, it seemed. Jordan held my purse out into my hands. That was when I noticed that they were practically carrying Tiffany on their shoulder. I tucked the card into my bag and helped Jordan walk Tiffany out of the building.

I'd offered to drive everyone home since I hadn't drunk as much as they had, and there was no way Tiffany could have waited for a car service to pick them up from the corner. After the interruption from being caught up in Stolas, I was stone-cold sober.

Tiffany sulked in the back seat during the drive to her apartment, huffing and whining that Rhomi had ruined the night that could have changed her life. The guy she had been dancing—or rather dry-humping—with had been whispering promises in her ear all night. When Rhomi freaked out on Oro, Tiffany hadn't had time to get his name or number.

Jordan offered to stay with Tiffany and assured us that they would tuck Tiffany in with a large water bottle and call Rhomi in the morning.

Rhomi still lived with her father in the Hills. His house was twice the size of my father's and surrounded by a stone wall.

Rhomi punched in the code for the gate then asked down to my car window, "Do you want to stay the night? It would be like old times."

I'd had enough of trying to relive our past friendship. I wanted to get out of this dress and wash my face.

"Thanks, but I should get back home. I have a long day tomorrow."

She pouted her lips then stood up fully. "Okay, but don't be a stranger. Shopping next week. It's a demand."

I smiled and watched her walk through her gate up to the front door before I backed out of her driveway and headed home.

It was another night of driving the streets of L.A. alone and heading back to an empty apartment with a vague plan to possibly see someone outside of work that felt more like an obligation than an adventure. I was second-guessing my choice to come back more and more. But that caged feeling around my lungs constricted to remind me that I had no other choice. This was my existence because it had to be.

T was making myself breakfast when my phone flashed my father's name on an incoming call.

"Hey, Dad. What's up?" I said around a mouthful of oatmeal.

"Evelyn, I got a call from an associate this morning telling me that he saw you at one of those sleazy nightclubs last night with Oro. You better have a good explanation as to why you would be hanging around a grown man at a nightclub."

"If it was so sleazy, why was your associate there in the first place?" I snipped back, setting my bowl down on the counter. I leaned against it to wait for his rebuttal.

"Don't take that tone with me," he scolded. "How could you be so careless with my campaign on the line?"

"I'm an adult whether your public knows it or not. And I didn't go there with Oro. I went with some friends. We ran into him and his brothers there. That's it."

The anger bubbling to my skin's surface rattled my core. The last time he'd yelled at me was when I was home on a holiday break from school and backed into a parking meter with his new car. That was years ago, yet the tone in his voice brought me right back to feeling like a stupid, careless teenager.

"Stay away from Oro and his whole company. Family. Whatever they are. They are not good people."

My head pounded as reason found its way to my tongue. "Then why do you know them well enough to invite them to your fundraiser at your home?"

"They have deep pockets, but their hands are as dirty as they come. This discussion is over. Never again, do you hear me?"

I didn't answer.

I hung up and slammed the phone facedown on the kitchen counter. A sigh dragged out of me and built into a frustrated shout. It bounced off the walls of my kitchen and into the living room before it faded to silence. I marched to my room and got dressed, determined to escape my own mind for a couple hours.

Before leaving, I grabbed the purse I'd had with me at the club last night and pulled out my wallet. With it came the small matte-black card.

Sy Luxe
The Deacon
Owner

On the back were three words that looked to be Latin.

Loquere, et introire

Was this the invitation that Rhomi had talked about and the item Jordan had flashed at the beginning of the night?

It didn't matter.

After last night and the call with my father, I had no intention of going back to The Deacon. There was something childish and embarrassing about being rushed out of a club because of a friend's altercation. I could still feel Stolas' hand making its way up my thigh.

I got in my car and drove toward the coast, needing to escape into the shallow waves.

Maybe God would take pity on me and a shark

would take me out before I could disappoint my father or see Stolas again.

A girl could dream.

13

STOLAS

I f my trainer hadn't been demonic, I would have killed them in my Monday morning session. Weights, cardio, sparring, then more cardio had been my way of wasting time.

Sunday had come and gone without a word from Evie, which meant that Orobas owed me money and that she hadn't canceled our date later.

At least not yet.

"I had a call from Harris Gerhardt a few minutes ago," Orobas said by way of greeting as he entered my office. He was thirty minutes late and carried two cups of coffee.

"Finally ready to give his own soul for the pursuit of power?" I scoffed and accepted the cup Orobas offered.

"He heard about Evie's trip to The Deacon Saturday night." Orobas lifted a brow. "He sounded quite enraged."

I had fed that information through the right channels. I'd seen one of Harris' closest and slimiest associates in one of the other VIP booths after Evie left and made sure the moment we'd shared was broadcasted.

"He's disappointed in her for keeping us as company. I tasted a hint of wrath in his tone. Decadent."

"Good, then he's close to his breaking point," I said, going back to my laptop.

"If you say so." Orobas disappeared behind my door and left me to work.

I checked my phone every few minutes for any word from Evie on the matter.

Knowing politicians, Harris had warned her off from Orobas and me, but the closer it got to five o'clock, the more my confidence grew that Evie was a rebellious heart and transfixed with her own desires. I was getting attached to the idea of keeping Evie in more ways than one.

As I was readying myself to leave the office to meet Evie for our dinner, Haniel appeared holding the locket I'd intended to return to her.

He was weathered, gray, and balding. His appearance over the years had shifted with the use of his magic and many failed attempts at darker alchemy. He'd lost bits of flesh from his fingers to explosions in his workshop. Some things could not be undone, even for immortal beings.

He held out the necklace by its chain. "The

trinket is bonded and ready for its owner, Your Highness."

I held out my hand. The weight of the locket had been altered slightly, and the cool chain snaked between the creases of my fingers. Evie may not notice the shift in the locket itself, but the chain would no longer warm against her skin after seconds of being worn. Living in Southern California, that would be an oddity, but she'd likely explain it away in her head before thinking to take it off since it held more sentimental value than most pieces Haniel worked on.

"Thank you. My payment has been deposited into your account, and I've sent you a pretty little gift for your swiftness on this piece," I said, shifting my hand for the light to catch on the glints of gold on the locket's hinge.

"You're too kind, my most powerful liege." His grainy voice dissipated as he stepped back through the void to where he would find the thirty-five-year-old bottle of Irish whiskey and a lesser demon from my legion to do with as he pleased.

I was about half a block away from the restaurant when I spotted Evie waiting outside the front door. If she had come from work, it didn't show. Her soft, bouncy curls weren't weighed down by a day's worth of anxious raking from her fingers. Her lipstick wasn't smudged by the lids of coffee cups. She was perfect.

She checked her watch then panned the passing crowd until she caught sight of me. A faint smile of relief crested her lips before she masked it, robbing me of the smug satisfaction that came from being the highlight of her day. Feeling utterly slighted, I met her at the door and offered my arm to start the date I intended to finish with her legs wrapped around my hips.

The lobby of the building was split. The first two floors were for the luxury hotel, spa, and guests. The elevator to the restaurant on the rooftop did not stop for any other floors to give guests privacy.

As luck would have it, the elevator was empty when Evie and I got onto it. She pressed her back against the wall and gave a heavy sigh when the doors closed.

"Long day?" I asked, lighting the button to the roof with a jab of my finger.

I turned to find she looked more relaxed than when we'd met on the street.

"It was, but to be honest, I've had a lot of people around me all day. It's just nice to have a moment of silence." She noted the curiosity on my face then gave me a smile that felt more genuine than any I'd experienced in too many years. "With you."

My fingers drummed against the cold metal railing behind me. I wanted to pull her into my chest, breathe in the floral scent of her hair, and beg to be the solace she needed at the end of an exhausting day. But there was a reason I chose this restaurant, and he wasn't here yet.

The doors opened, and the sprawling patio garden welcomed us out into the evening air. Weaving my fingers through hers, I led the way to the table I'd reserved, which was in direct sight of the senator's favorite seat at the bar.

It wasn't hard to pass time with Evie. She enjoyed her job and recanted the reconnection she'd attempted with the friend who'd brought her to The Deacon a couple nights earlier.

"Oro got off easy." She laughed comfortably through her story. "Once in high school, Rhomi's father came to our economics class and threatened to sue a guy who had stood Rhomi up for prom."

"What was he accusing him of?"

"Emotional distress and loss of value for the dress he bought her."

She squeezed my wrist as we laughed.

"I am sorry for my brother. He doesn't know the meaning of moderation." My excuse was far from acceptable. Orobas knew better than to force himself on a human with so many witnesses around.

"He does seem to have a track record of not being able to resist his urges. That's going to get him into a lot of trouble someday," she warned.

"My brothers have a way of finding trouble."

At the mention of the other princes, she squirmed in her seat. "About Sy." Her cheeks reddened. "I didn't know he was your brother and—"

"Unless you're about to give me a reason to bloody his nose, you have nothing to worry about."

Her embarrassment for being entranced by Sitri was useless. I held no ill feelings toward her or my brother. She was beautiful. And he was pure human desire. In fact, I found it telling that she was still interested in seeing me at all after meeting Sitri. It was difficult not allowing that to go to my head.

She didn't need to answer with anything more than the tight-lipped smile and nod before we moved on to the topic of what we were going to order for dinner.

When she excused herself to the bathroom, I moved our chairs closer together. I could have told myself that I was setting the scene for Harris, but it would've been a half truth. I wanted her scent on my skin and to hear her breath hitch when she caught me smiling at her wit. As if she shared my desire, she returned and scooted her chair even closer until our knees were touching and my hands easily slipped over her thigh.

"I always wanted to go to Paris." She paused

between bites and sentences for short sips of her wine. "But once I got to London, I spent the first year learning to drive on the right side of the road."

"I never drive internationally for that very reason." My thumb caressed the top of her knee, encouraging her further.

"It's so much harder than it looks, but I'll never get used to the Channel Tunnel."

I hung on her every word and immersed myself in her world. She loved to travel, and I could take her away from Los Angeles, away from the expectations of her ruthless father.

During our first dessert, Evie ordered a custard pastry and made a sound that instantly made me jealous of a cream puff. She sucked the vanilla-bean-spotted cream from her spoon and ignited visions of other things I wanted her to suck so seductively.

She caught me staring and smiled at the heat in my eyes, disarming me once again. I shook the feeling away, and when I looked back at her, she leaned in to press her lips to mine.

Restraint warred with every natural impulse that coursed through my body. It took every ounce of willpower I'd gained in the Fall to not take her on top of the table after I saw the coy satisfaction on her face for making the first move. The sight of Harris' daughter bent over in front of the entire bar would have been worth the slip of my original plans.

Evie cleared her throat and took another forkful

of dessert, licking the sweet custard from the prongs and sending a signal straight to my dick.

She would be mine. After her father knew she was no longer his pawn to play.

The sun had long since disappeared beyond the horizon when the man of the hour finally arrived with his trophy wife on his arm and several local politicians at his back.

I knew I shouldn't have, but the prudence I'd once possessed had departed with my third glass of wine over a second dessert. The slow caresses of my fingers over her skin had brought her walls down, and her father was now seeing his daughter practically purring in my lap.

His face fell and drained of its color, and I could almost see the thirst for my blood in his eyes. I half expected him to storm over and rip her from her chair, but his diplomacy won out over his fatherly instincts. His wife pulled at the crook of his arm, and after a quick pause, he followed her to their reserved seats.

Evie, who had been taking the last sip from her glass, caught the cruel glee on my face. Puzzled, she looked around to find what had stolen my attention away for the first time all night.

"Is that . . . ," she whispered, worried that her voice would carry and direct her father's crew toward us. "I have to go."

"Wait," I said with little enthusiasm as she gathered her things.

She got to her feet and made a quick beeline to the exit, doing exactly what I wanted her to do. Harris caught sight of her and excused himself to trail after her. I took my time retrieving three hundred-dollar bills from my wallet and handing them to our waiter before I joined Evie and her father at the doors of the summoned elevator.

"What are you doing here with him? He's dangerous. You have no idea what you've done—what you're risking," he scolded, red-faced and flustered.

"It was one date. I'm a grown woman, and I can make my own choices—"

"Is everything all right?" I slipped into their hushed conversation.

Harris pointed an accusatory finger at me. "Get away from her, you snake. I warned your idiot brother—"

"Watch your temper, Gerhardt, your constituents are watching," I said, peering over my shoulder at the small crowd of turned heads behind us.

At the lift's chime, Harris grabbed Evie by the elbow, pulling her inside before she could vocalize the apology brewing in her tear-lined eyes.

I smiled wolfishly as the doors closed. Harris Gerhardt was about to implode the last relationship that was worth his soul.

I took the emergency stairwell down to the ground floor to lie in wait for Evie.

14

EVIE

Embarrassment flooded my face as my dad pulled me away from Stolas, who watched with what looked like annoyance mixed with a calm knowing.

Did he know my dad would be here tonight?

"You should be ashamed of yourself, Evelyn. Slobbering all over that monster in public like a whore."

Shock and ice plunged into my stomach. My dad had never spoken to me like that, not even in my rebellious teenage years.

"What did you just say?" The words came out weak and shaky as I fought to hold back tears.

"He's a demon. And I don't mean that figuratively." His anger vibrated the walls around us.

"You're insane. He's been nothing but kind to me since I met him."

The doors had barely opened when I rushed

125

through them. I needed to get away from him as fast as I could before he made a scene in the lobby.

"Evelyn!" he shouted after me. "Come back here."

I shoved past two men coming through the front door and took off down the sidewalk to the parking lot around the corner. Even if my dad did follow, he wouldn't risk anyone seeing him chase down my car on foot. I turned the next corner but slammed into a solid chest.

"Evie, there you are," Stolas said, not at all out of breath.

His hands wrapped around my upper arms and pulled me farther into the shadows of the building. The car lot was across the street, illuminated by yellowed street lamps and passing headlights. The urge to bolt out into traffic was hard to ignore, but Stolas' hands held me firm against the cool brick.

"Stolas, I don't know what is going on between you and my dad, but I don't want to be a part of it. If you asked me out to get under his skin or blackmail him—"

I choked on my emotions and could feel the tears falling down my cheeks. Their hot and traitorous streams were hard to hide even in the darkness of the night.

"He told you, but you don't believe him." His deep voice crowded closer as he dipped his chin to the top of my head.

"He told me you were evil. That you were a monster."

"I am."

I blinked up at him through the tears.

What was he saying? Was he admitting that he was just using me to piss off my dad?

"I never claimed to be a good man, Evie, but he told you something else."

His eyes somehow brightened.

It had to be a reflection from a passing car, or maybe the overhead lamp post at the end of the block, but the heat under his fingers grew painful against my skin and the dull glow behind his eyes grew brighter until I was gasping for air.

"Demon," I managed to breathe out. "He said you were a demon."

"That's right. And do you know why he knows what I am? What could a popular politician have to gain from being friendly with a demonic presence?"

He was leading me to the answer, showing me what he wanted me to work out on my own.

My father had always been a likable and social man, but there had been defining moments in his life that had built up his career and catapulted him from local government, up to the state level, then on to Washington, D.C. The passing of my mother and siblings was the only major circumstance he'd faced, but I couldn't believe that my dad had anything to do with that. I wouldn't believe it.

127

"Say it out loud, Evie." Stolas' gruff voice was laced with eager tolerance.

"No." I wiggled my shoulders, trying to break free of his hold, but his body pushed me harder into the wall at my back.

"You're so close to the truth. I know you can see it. It's on the tip of your tongue. The buried memory of a familiar face before the accident." He coaxed me with words and a hand down my side to my hip.

My memories around that time were fuzzy at best. But that day would be seared into my brain forever, though there were chunks of time before and after that grief had robbed me of. My mother's funeral was a blur, as was the dedication ceremony of a park in my family's honor. I could only see flashes when I thought my hardest to piece those events together.

"Think back. Weeks before that day," Stolas instructed. His hand cupped the back of my knee, hitching my leg on his hip.

His breath on my neck and lips on my ear lobe distracted me from the pain of remembering what he needed me to see.

The face in my father's office about a month before my mother, brother, and sister would die on the brand-new boat.

That cunning grin and cutting, odd wit.

"We have a deal then?" the dark voice says.

I'm watching from the crack in the door, crouched like

a spy while my brother counts downstairs. I need to find a hiding place before he gets to one hundred, but the way our dad is sitting has my eyes glued to him.

"I have your word. They won't feel any pain and it'll be quick?" My dad's voice comes up from his desk, but his face is covered by his hands.

"Not even a pinch. Three little souls for the next step to the White House." The other man flicks lint from his shoulder then checks his watch.

"Just three. No more. No less," my father agrees, finally looking up to the face of . . .

"Oro." My voice was hoarse and strained from the tension and pressure that had been building in my body.

"What did Oro and your father do?" Stolas' lips moved over the sensitive spot under my jaw.

"They . . . They made a deal. He's a demon, too. Just like . . ." I allowed the realization to wash over me.

"Me?"

My stomach turned into knots as he lifted me and settled his hips between my legs for our eyes to meet. I knew I should have been afraid, but we'd been alone for hours before my dad had shown up. How could Stolas have been some otherworldly monster without me knowing it? Or was I so cut off from humanity by my own bitter loneliness that I couldn't see the devil dancing before my eyes?

"Evie, I'm not going to hurt you," he said, a softness to his voice that I hadn't heard before, hadn't needed to hear yet. "I know it may be difficult to understand, but I want to help you. I need you to trust me."

"You're a demon! You're vile and evil."

"What makes me more vile than any other being? How is my existence any more evil than the men who rape their own children or policy makers who willingly allow thousands of people to drink tainted water with no resolution?"

His body warmed my skin. I should have been thrashing to get away from him, but I couldn't will myself to move.

My arms circled his neck, and I pulled myself into him, wanting him closer.

He adjusted my weight, and I felt his stiffening excitement press harder between my thighs. "Books written by men who committed some of the greatest sins known to man are never seen as monstrous as I. I can assure you that my hands have never been so bloodied as those wearing an alb."

He didn't sound upset, and the swell in his pants sure as fuck didn't feel like anger. His hand slipped under my skirt and pulled my panties to the side to allow his fingers to caress the pool of throbbing heat.

"He's hurt you in ways that I could never heal, but I would rip him apart, limb by limb, for you. Just say the word."

He was talking about my dad. The man who raised me for slaughter.

Three souls. Not four. I was Harris Gerhardt's last poker chip. That was why he didn't want me getting close to Stolas. He didn't want me giving myself to a demon before it was the most opportune time for his legacy. But there I was, on a dark L.A. street, my pussy aching and my eyes flooding with tears.

I'd known my own grief longer than I'd known most people, yet Stolas ushered me to confront a truth that I hadn't known I was missing. A secret that burned in my core and opened a wound that should have had me unraveling. I heard the click of metal, then the down stroke of a zipper.

The head of his engorged cock nudged my entrance. Was I really about to let a demon fuck me right out in the open?

"Stolas." I didn't have words, just his name and the slow build of his fingers brushing over my clit to the rhythm of his breath over my chest.

"Please, Evie," he said between my breasts. "Fuck. I need you."

What he was asking for was more than my consent. He had that already, and he knew it.

What he wanted was me. All of me. He needed me to say it out loud, for me to offer myself willingly.

But for what?

With nothing left and everything to risk, I rolled my hips over his thick, wet tip.

He groaned and took in a deep breath. I could feel his restraint and the surge of what I was about to unleash. This ancient creature was waiting on my words, and that sort of power sent my head swimming.

His hips pulsed, and I shed one last tear for Harris Gerhardt and the family that had been stolen from me. Stolas' lips sucked at my collarbone, and he shook with another deep sound of desperation.

"I'm yours."

The air shot from my lungs as he pushed inside of me.

He was too big. I was already filled to my tipping point, throbbing around him. I tightened my grip around his neck for balance.

He groaned as he spread me wider.

I whimpered through gritted teeth, an orgasm ready to crash through me with the slightest change in pressure. He waited for me to adjust to his thick shaft, and my walls constricted around him. His fingers dug into my ass as he drew his hips back, then plunged into me and brought me down to his base.

"Oh God." All my restraint to be quiet was gone as the orgasm gripped my lower belly.

"You belong to *me*," he practically growled in my ear. "I will be your salvation."

His thrusts deepened with each withdrawal. And with every grind of his hips came his name from my lips, louder and louder.

My voice echoed off the surrounding buildings.

Anyone who walked or drove by could have seen

us, and that terror would have normally mortified me but sent a thrill through me now.

Stolas looked up for the first time, locking his determined gaze with mine. "Pray to me, Evie, and I will give you everything."

My body was weak and shaking, but his almost begging tone whirled in my core.

He wrapped his arms around the small of my back, bringing it off the rough surface of the building we had made into a place of passion and need. When I was firmly seated around his hips, he circled, his pelvis grinding against my overworked clit.

"Fuck, Stolas," I panted.

As I felt his cock pulse and jerk deep inside of me, I cried out, begged him not to stop, and finally hit the epitome of pleasure. My hips bucked, and I rode out the orgasm as he moaned and gritted out my name until his shoulders sagged and his head fell to my panting chest.

When he looked up through spent, hooded eyes, I felt the swell in my chest—a gratitude I couldn't explain for the act we had just committed.

He gently placed me on my feet and quickly zipped his pants while I righted my clothes. His body hardly left mine before he took me into his arms and held me close, like he couldn't bare the distance. Breathing him in, I tried—and failed—to imagine a world where he was still just human. Knowing that he wasn't should have made my skin crawl, but I could only feel the warmth of his touch that soothed something deep and broken inside of me.

The smell of his sweat and cologne on my skin filled my lungs. Spice, musk, and sex. My new favorite scent.

"Evie?" he pleaded.

My throat tightened, though not with sadness or tears. "Take me to him."

15

STOLAS

I would never be the same. The undying thirst had been quenched, and not by blood or power. It was a combination of things in the end. One was the way Evie held her head high and drew strength from her pain. The next was having the privilege of standing at her side as she took what was owed to her by her father.

Her life for her own.

His office was dark when he stumbled in an hour after we'd arrived. Evie sat behind his desk in the plush leather chair, her hand firmly wrapped around her mother's locket. Both she and the trinket were reborn and under my protection.

"Evelyn?" Harris' eyes darted between me and his daughter. "What's this all about?"

"I'm giving you a chance to explain yourself." Her voice was firm and direct.

"He's a monster, kitten, you can't trust a thing he says," Harris said.

Harris was a trapped rat. He had traded all three of his children's souls that day. But as fate would have it, their mother had perished instead of Evie. Perhaps it was a sleight of hand by her mother's Reaper that saved Evie's life.

"You're going to have to do better than that, Gerhardt," I chided.

From where I stood, I could see the panic and rage wash over him. "If you don't think I know who to call to get rid of you and your bastard brothers, you're underestimating me."

The threat surged my blood. "I'd rethink your tactic. You're not in the position to make promises you can't keep," I volleyed.

He scowled but didn't dare argue. If it were up to me, he wouldn't make it out of this room with his mortal life.

"Dad. I know what you did." Evie got to her feet and rounded the desk to meet his eyes. "I need to know that you didn't trade our family just for politics."

Harris paused. His last blood relative stood before him confronting him with more than his lies, sins, and deepest regrets. Evie was baring her pain to him for the first time in a new light. They were finally seeing each other for who they had become by the consequences of his actions.

"I knew I could make a difference, not just for

our family but for the world. I was born for greatness, power, and to make real change. One small moment set all of this in motion." He gestured to the room around us in a vague attempt to justify his choices.

"This life was worth your children and wife?" Evie's tear-strained voice shook. "Sacrificing our lives and souls for a chance at the White House?"

"I did what I had to do. Duty and honor had to come above all else."

It was the last nail in the coffin for Harris Gerhardt. He'd squandered his only chance to talk himself back into her good graces and save himself from my wrath.

Evie's shoulders rose as her lungs filled with stale disappointment. I stepped to her side and placed my hand on her lower back. Her muscles tensed, but her next words held the strength I'd hoped my show of solidarity would inspire.

"You had a duty to protect your family," she said, her tone lethal. "And I will spend the rest of my life honoring them by exposing you for the stone-hearted fraud you are. Not one of your achievements will be saved from the stains of your betrayals."

"No one will believe you. Angels. Demons. You may as well be spouting about aliens."

"You can keep that truth to yourself. I have plenty of others to share," she countered.

"Many supplied by me," I interjected. "The perk

of working so closely with your many high-powered campaign donors."

"There's no proof." Harris narrowed his eyes at the both of us. "Not a single paper trail would lead to me."

"You're forgetting the kind of influence I have over humans. What I could promise for a few small favors." I gave him a crooked smile to remind him of what I really was.

"And what am I supposed to do, then? What about all the good I have done for the community?" He was starting to scramble. "The charities or beautification projects that I personally founded to make this state a better place? Were those things for nothing?"

"The thing about ambition is that it can be blinding," I said. I looked down at Evie and cupped her cheek to bring her eyes to mine for a moment before finishing my last point to Harris. We both needed the moment of connection. "No matter how good your intentions are, you've done it out of your own selfishness, not for the betterment of your own kind. You've tainted them all."

"You're going to resign from all public positions," Evie said, beginning her list of demands. "Tell them that you've decided to pledge your life working with nonprofits. And every day, until the day you're too old and decrepit, you're going to volunteer in the name of the family you slaughtered."

"Evelyn—"

"You owe me a soul, dad." She was finished listening to him. "You're going to earn the clemency you reserved for yourself away from the spotlight you've craved my entire life."

"Make the announcement in the morning or I'll be back to assist you," I added.

Evie turned into my chest, and with that signal, I took us through the void to my home.

Through everything, Evie still loved her father, and who was I to fault her for that.

She'd granted him a kindness that grated on my nerves, but for her sake, a slow burn from the public eye would be the best precursor for the punishments he would receive in Hell.

I couldn't return her soul to her—the laws of balance would never allow it—but I could take care of her and keep her safe for the rest of her days on this plane, then for an eternity after.

16

"Why me?"

It felt like a foolish question that I already knew the answer to. I stroked the wings of the owl tattoo sprawled across his bare chest.

After leaving my father in shambles in his office, Stolas brought us to his house in Santa Monica. I'd taken two steps inside before his mouth crashed over mine and our clothes were on the floor. We made it to his bed and hadn't left since.

The sun was now rising and filling his bedroom with bright, golden rays that held more than a new day. Rest wasn't something I could bring myself to do. The full weight of what I'd done to my father and the sadness for myself came in waves. Between my fits of tears and rage was Stolas. Every doubt I voiced, he soothed. When reality felt like too much, he chased it away with passion.

"Because you've done the unthinkable." He rolled onto his side then pulled his body over mine. "You've satiated me. You're everything I've ever needed and more."

"That's hard to believe," I said, my cheeks flushing.

"My existence has been plagued with the pursuit of things I could never possess. The power I thought I craved would have destroyed me, and chasing it made me a monster."

He leaned down, kissed me deeply, and stole my breath once again. "It took one night with you to realize what I really needed was someone worth existing for. And in return, I'm going to love you in ways only the Prince of Greed can."

"I look forward to it."

And for the first time in too many years, I felt whole. As impossible as it was, I knew we belonged together.

THE END

POP
MY
CHERRY

🍒 **2 OZ AGED SMOKED WHISKEY**

🍒 **1 LARGE ICE CUBE**

🍒 **.5 OZ SIMPLE SYRUP**

🍒 **FINISH WITH ALCOHOL MARINATED CHERRY**

ACKNOWLEDGMENTS

Thank you to A. K. Mulford for always being my
bookish wifey! I don't know what I would do without
you. Cry. I would cry.
A special thanks to my Hype Team for being so
supportive and making me smile every day. You're all
so incredible!

Made in the USA
Columbia, SC
28 September 2024

43145682R10095